THE POTTER'S FIELD

Andrea Camilleri was one of Italy's most famous contemporary writers. The Inspector Montalbano series, which has sold over 65 million copies worldwide, has been translated into thirty-two languages and was adapted for Italian television, screened on BBC4. *The Potter's Field*, the thirteenth book in the series, was awarded the Crime Writers' Association's International Dagger for the best crime novel translated into English. In addition to his phenomenally successful Inspector Montalbano series, he was also the author of the historical comic mysteries *Hunting Season* and *The Brewer of Preston*. He died in Rome in July 2019.

Stephen Sartarelli is an award-winning translator. He is also the author of three books of poetry, most recently *The Open Vault*. He lives in France.

Also by Andrea Camilleri

Inspector Montalbano mysteries

Short Stories

Other Novels

ANDREA CAMILLERI

THE POTTER'S FIELD

Translated by Stephen Sartarelli

PICADOR

First published 2011 by Penguin Books US,
an imprint of Penguin Random House LLC

First published in the UK 2012 by Mantle

This edition published 2021 by Picador
an imprint of Pan Macmillan
The Smithson, 6 Briset Street, London EC1M 5NR
EU representative: Macmillan Publishers Ireland Ltd,
Mallard Lodge, Lansdowne Village, Dublin 4
Associated companies throughout the world
www.panmacmillan.com

ISBN 978-1-5290-4388-4

Copyright © Sellerio Editore 2008
Translation copyright © Stephen Sartarelli 2011

Originally published in Italian 2012 as *Il campo del vasaio* by Sellerio Editore, Palermo

The right of Andrea Camilleri to be identified as the
author of this work has been asserted by him in accordance
with the Copyright, Designs and Patents Act 1988.

Pan Macmillan does not have any control over, or any responsibility for,
any author or third-party websites referred to in or on this book.

1 3 5 7 9 8 6 4 2

A CIP catalogue record for this book is available from the British Library.

Printed and bound by CPI Group (UK) Ltd, Croydon, CR0 4YY

MIX
Paper from
responsible sources
FSC® C116313

Visit **www.panmacmillan.com** to read more about all our books
and to buy them. You will also find features, author interviews and
news of any author events, and you can sign up for e-newsletters
so that you're always first to hear about our new releases.

THE POTTER'S FIELD

ONE

He was awakened by a loud, insistent knocking at the door. A frantic knocking, with hands and feet but, curiously, no ringing of the doorbell. He looked over at the window. No dawn light filtered through the closed shutter; outside was still total darkness. Or, rather, every so often a treacherous flash lit up the window, chilling the room, followed by a thunderclap that shook the windowpanes. The storm that had started the day before was raging with greater fury than ever. Strangely, however, the surging sea was silent, though it must have eaten up the beach all the way to the veranda. He groped around on the bedside table, hand searching for the base of the small lamp. He pressed the button, clicking it twice, but the light didn't come on. Had the bulb burned out, or was there no electricity? He got up out of bed, a cold shudder running down his spine. Through the shutter slats came not only flashes of lightning, but blades of cold wind. The main light switch was also not working. Maybe the storm had knocked out the power.

The knocking continued. Amidst the pandemonium, he thought he heard a voice cry out, as if in distress.

'I'm coming! I'm coming!' he shouted.

Since he had been sleeping naked, he looked around for something to cover himself, but found nothing. He was sure he had left his trousers on the chair at the foot of the bed. Perhaps they had slid to the floor. But he had no time to waste. He ran to the front door.

'Who is it?' he asked before opening.

'Bonetti-Alderighi. Open up, hurry!'

He balked, utterly confused. The commissioner? What the hell was going on? Was this some kind of stupid joke?

'Just a moment.'

He ran to get the torch he kept in the kitchen-table drawer, switched it on, and opened the door. He could only gawk, stunned, at the rain-soaked commissioner standing before him. Bonetti-Alderighi was wearing a black, rumpled hat and a raincoat with a shredded left sleeve.

'Let me in,' he said.

Montalbano stepped aside and his boss came in. The inspector followed him mechanically, as if sleepwalking, forgetting to close the door, which started banging in the wind. Reaching the first chair at hand, the commissioner did not so much sit down as collapse in it. Before Montalbano's astonished eyes, he buried his face in his hands and started crying.

The questions in the inspector's mind began to accelerate like a jet before take-off, arising and vanishing too fast for him to catch hold of one that was clear and precise. He couldn't even open his mouth.

'Could you hide me here at your house?' the commissioner asked him anxiously.

Hide him? Why on earth would the commissioner need to hide? Was he a fugitive from justice? What had he done? Who was looking for him?

'I don't ... understand ...'

Bonetti-Alderighi looked at him in disbelief.

'What, Montalbano, do you mean you haven't heard?'

'No, I haven't.'

'The Mafia took power tonight!'

'What are you saying?!'

'Well, how else did you expect our wretched country to end up? A little change in the law here, a little change there, and here we are. Could I please have a glass of water?'

'Yes ... of course.'

He quickly realized the commissioner wasn't quite right in the head. Perhaps he'd had a car accident and was raving from the shock. The best thing was to call Montelusa Central Police. Or maybe it was better to call a doctor at once. Meanwhile, however, he mustn't let the poor man suspect anything. So, for the moment, at least, he had to humour him.

The inspector went into the kitchen and instinctively flipped the light switch. And the light came on. He filled a glass, turned to go back, and froze in the doorway, paralysed. He was a statue, the kind they make nowadays, which could have been called *Naked Man with Glass in Hand*.

The room was lit up, but the commissioner was no longer there. Sitting in his place was a short, stocky man with a *coppola* on his head, whom Montalbano recognized at once. Totò Riina! He'd been freed from prison! So Bonetti-Alderighi hadn't gone mad after all! What he'd said was the unvarnished truth!

'Evenin',' said Riina. 'Sorry to burst in on you like dis, an' at dis hour, but I don't got much time, and ousside dere's a 'elicopter waitin' a take me to Rome to form the new guv'ment. I already got a few names: Bernardo Provenzano for Vice-President, one of the Caruana brothers for Foreign Minister, Leoluca Bagarella at Defence ... So I come here wit' one quession for you, Inspector Montalbano, an' you gotta tell me yes or no straightaway. You wanna be my Minister of the Interior?'

But before Montalbano could answer, Catarella appeared in the room. He must have come in through the open front door. He was holding a revolver in his hand and aiming it at the inspector. Big tears rolled down his cheeks.

'Chief, if you say yes to this 'ere criminal, I'm gonna kill you poissonally in poisson!'

Talking, however, distracted Catarella, and Riina, quick as a snake, whipped out his own gun and fired. The light in the room went out, and . . .

*

Montalbano woke up. The only real thing in the dream he'd just had was the storm rattling the shutters, which he'd left open. He got up and closed them, then got back into bed after looking at the clock. Four in the morning. He wanted to seize hold of sleep again, but found himself arguing with the other Montalbano behind his stubbornly closed eyes.

'What was the meaning of that dream?'

'Why do you want to find a meaning in it, Montalbà? Don't you very often have dreams that don't mean a damn thing?'

'That's what you think, because you're an ignorant beast. They may mean nothing to you, but go tell that to Dr Freud, and you'll see what he can pull out of them!'

'But why should I tell my dreams to Dr Freud?'

'Because if you're unable to explain your dream, or have it explained to you, you'll never get back to sleep.'

'Oh, all right. Ask me a question.'

'Of all the things in the dream, what made the strongest impression on you?'

'The change.'

'Which one?'

5

'The one where I come out of the kitchen and find Totò Riina in Bonetti-Alderighi's place.'

'Explain.'

'Well, in the place of the representative of the law, there's the numero uno of the Mafia, the boss of people who are against the law.'

'So, what you're telling me is that in your own living room, in your own home, there with all your things, you found yourself playing host to the law and to people against the law.'

'So what?'

'Could it be that in your mind the boundary between the law and the anti-law has been getting a little blurrier each day?'

'Don't talk such crap!'

'All right, let's look at it another way. What did they ask of you?'

'Bonetti-Alderighi asked me to help him, to hide him at my house.'

'And did that surprise you?'

'Of course!'

'And what did Riina ask you?'

'He asked me to be his Minister of the Interior.'

'And did that surprise you?'

'Well, yes.'

'Did it surprise you as much as the commissioner's question? Or did it surprise you more? Or less? Answer sincerely.'

'Well, no, it surprised me less.'

'Why less? Do you consider it normal that a Mafia boss should ask you to work for him?'

'No, that's not how I would put it. Riina, at that moment, wasn't a Mafia boss any longer, he was about to become Prime

Minister! And it was as Prime Minister that he asked me to work for him.'

'Hold it right there. There are two ways to look at this. Either you think that the fact of someone's becoming Prime Minister cancels out all his prior crimes, murders and massacres included, or else you belong to that category of policemen who always serve, no matter what, whoever happens to be in power, whether an honest man or a criminal, whether a Fascist or a Communist. To which of these two categories do you belong?'

'Wait a minute! That's too easy!'

'Why do you say that?'

'Because then Catarella appeared!'

'And what does that mean?'

'It means, in fact, that I said no to Riina's offer.'

'But you didn't even open your mouth!'

'I said it through Catarella. He pops up, points his gun at me, and tells me he'll kill me if I accept. It's as if Catarella was my conscience.'

'Now there's something new from you! Catarella, your conscience?'

'Why not? Do you remember the time that journalist asked me if I believed in my guardian angel? When I answered yes, he asked me if I'd ever seen him. And I said yes, I see him every day. "Does he have a name?" the journalist asked. And without missing a beat, I said, "His name is Catarella." I was joking, of course. But later on, after thinking it over, I realized that only a small part of it was in jest, and the rest was the truth.'

'Conclusion?'

'The question should be read in the opposite way. The scene with Catarella means that rather than accept Riina's offer, I was ready to shoot myself.'

'Are you sure, Montalbà, that Freud would have interpreted it this way?'

'You know what I say to you? That I don't give a flying fuck about Freud. Now let me get some sleep, I can hardly keep my eyes open any more.'

*

When he woke up it was already past nine. He didn't see or hear any lightning or thunder, but the weather certainly was nasty outside. Why bother to get up? His two old wounds ached. And a few little pains, unpleasant companions of his age, had awakened with him. He was better off sleeping for another couple of hours. He got up, went into the dining room, unplugged the phone, went back to bed, pulled up the covers, and closed his eyes.

*

Barely half an hour later he opened them again, awakened by the phone's insistent ringing. But how the hell could the phone be ringing if he'd unplugged it? And if it wasn't the phone, what was it? The doorbell, idiot! He felt a kind of engine oil, dense and viscous, circulating in his brain. Seeing his trousers on the floor, he put them on and went to the door, cursing the saints.

It was Catarella, out of breath.

'Ahh, Chief, Chief!'

'Listen, don't tell me anything, don't talk at all. I'll tell you when you can open your mouth. I'm going to get back into bed, and you're going to go into the kitchen, brew me a pot of good strong coffee, pour it all into a milk-bowl, put in three teaspoons of sugar, and bring it to me. Then you can tell me whatever it is you have to say.'

When Catarella returned with the steaming mug, he had to shake the inspector to wake him up. During those ten minutes he had fallen back into a deep sleep.

What is this, anyway? he thought as he was sipping his coffee, which tasted like reheated chicory broth. Isn't it well known that the older you get, the less sleep you need? So why is that in my case, the more the years go by, the more I sleep?

''Ow's the coffee taste, Chief?'

'Excellent, Cat.'

And he raced into the bathroom to rinse his mouth, for fear he might be sick.

'Cat, is this a pressing matter?'

'Relative, Chief.'

'All right, then, give me a few minutes to shower and get dressed.'

When he was all clean and dressed, he went into the kitchen and made himself a proper pot of coffee.

Going back into the dining room, he found Catarella

in front of the French windows that gave onto the veranda. He had opened the shutters.

It was pouring and the sea had come all the way up to the veranda, shaking it from time to time with the undertow of a particularly strong wave.

'C'n I talk now, Chief?' Catarella asked.

'Yes.'

'They found a dead body.'

Ah, what a discovery! What a find! Apparently the corpse of someone who'd died a 'white death' – the shorthand used by journalists when someone suddenly disappears without so much as saying goodbye – had resurfaced somewhere. But why give death any colour at all? White death! As if there were also a green death, a yellow death, and so on ... Actually, if one had to give death a colour, there could only be one: black, black as pitch.

'Is it fresh?'

'They din't say, Chief.'

'Where'd they find it?'

'Out inna country, Chief. Pizzutello districk.'

Imagine that. A desolate, godforsaken place, all sheer drops and jagged spurs, where a corpse could feel at home and never be discovered.

'Have any of our people been out to see it?'

'Yessir, Chief, Fazio and 'Spector Augello's at the premisses.'

'So why'd you come and bother *me*?'

'Chief, y'gotta unnastand, it was 'Spector Augello 'at call me and tell me to tell yiz yer poissonal presence 's 'ndisposable. An' so, seein' as how 's was no answer when I tried a call yiz onna phone, I took the Jeep and come out here poissonally in poisson.'

'Why'd you take the Jeep?'

'Cuz the reggler car coun't never make it to that place, Chief.'

'All right then, let's go.'

'Chief, 'e also tol' me to tell yiz iss bitter if y'put on some boots an' a raincoat, an som'n a cover y'head.'

The Catherine wheel of curses that burst from Montalbano's mouth left Catarella terrified.

*

The deluge showed no sign of letting up. They rolled along almost blindly, since the windscreen wipers were unable to sweep the water away. On top of this the last half-mile before reaching the spot where the corpse had been found was a cross between a roller coaster and an earthquake measuring 8.0 on the Richter scale. The inspector's bad mood deteriorated into a heavy silence and Catarella was so nervous he didn't miss a single pond-sized ditch.

'Did you remember to bring life jackets?'

Catarella didn't answer, only wishing he was the corpse they were going to see. At one point Montalbano's stomach turned upside down, bringing the nauseating taste of Catarella's coffee back up into his throat and mouth.

Finally, by the grace of God, they pulled up alongside the other Jeep, which Augello and Fazio had used. The only problem was that there was no sign anywhere of Augello or Fazio, or of any corpse whatsoever.

'Are we playing hide-and-seek or something?' Montalbano enquired.

'Chief, alls they tol' me was to stop as soon as I seen their Jeep.'

'Give them a toot.'

'A toot o' wha', Chief?'

'What the hell do you think, Cat? A toot of your trumpet? A toot of your tenor sax? Honk the horn!'

'The horn don' work, Chief.'

'Well, I guess that means we'll have to wait here till dark.'

He fired up a cigarette. By the time he'd finished it, Catarella had made up his mind.

'Chief, I'm gonna go look for 'em m'self. Seeing as how their Jeep's right here, maybe it means they're maybe right here, inna vinicity.'

'Take my raincoat.'

'Nah, Chief, I can't.'

'Why not?'

'Cuz a raincoat's civillan clothes 'n' I'm in uniform.'

'But who's going to see you here?'

'Chief, a uniform's always a uniform.'

He opened the door, got out, cried, 'Ah!' and vanished. He disappeared so quickly, in fact, that Montalbano feared he might have fallen into a ditch full of water and was drowning. So he quickly got out of the car himself, and in the twinkling of an eye found himself sliding arse first down a muddy slope some thirty feet long at the bottom of which sat Catarella, looking like a sculpture made out of fresh clay.

'I mussa parked the Jeep right aside the edge wittout realizin' it, Chief.'

'I realized that, Cat. So how are we going to climb out of here?'

'Look, Chief, see 'at little path over there, over onna left? I'm gonna go 'ave a look-see, 'n' you c'n follow me, but be real careful, cuz iss all slip'ry 'n' all.'

About fifty yards on, the path turned to the right. The heavy rain made it impossible to see even a short distance ahead. Suddenly Montalbano heard someone calling from above.

'Chief! We're over here!'

He looked up. Fazio was standing on top of a sort of elevation, reachable via three huge steps cut directly into the rock-face. He was sheltered under an enormous red-and-yellow umbrella of the kind shepherds use. Where on earth had he found it? To climb the three steps, Montalbano had to have Catarella push him from behind and Fazio pull him up by the hand.

I'm no longer cut out for this life, he thought bitterly.

The elevation turned out to be a tiny level clearing in front of the entrance to a cave that one could enter. Once inside, the inspector was wonderstruck.

It was warm in the cave. A fire was burning inside a circle of stones. A carter's oil-lamp hung from the vault and gave off sufficient light. A man of about sixty with a pipe in his mouth and Mimì were sitting on stools made of branches and playing cards on a little table between them, also made of branches. Every so often, taking turns, they took a sip from a flask of wine on the ground. A pastoral scene. Especially as there was no hint of the corpse anywhere. The sixtyish man greeted the inspector; Mimì did not. In fact, for the past month or so, Augello had been at odds with all of creation.

'The body was discovered by the man playing cards with Inspector Augello,' said Fazio, gesturing towards him. 'His name is Pasquale Ajena, and this is his land. He comes here every day. And he's equipped the cave so that he can eat here, rest here, or just sit here and look out at the landscape.'

'May I humbly ask where the hell the body is?'

'Apparently, Chief, it's about fifty yards further down.'

'*Apparently*? Are you saying you haven't seen it yet?'

'Yes. According to Mr Ajena, the spot is practically unreachable, unless it stops raining.'

'But this isn't going to stop before evening, if we're lucky!'

'There'll be a break in the clouds in about an hour,' Ajena cut in. 'Guaranteed, with a twist of lemon on it. And then it'll start raining again.'

'So what are we supposed to do till then?'

'Did you eat this morning?' Ajena asked him.

'No.'

'Would you like a little fresh tumazzo with a slice of wheat bread made yesterday?'

Montalbano's heart opened and let in a gentle breeze of contentment.

'I don't mind if I do.'

Ajena got up, opened a capacious haversack that was hanging from a nail, and pulled out a loaf of bread, a whole tumazzo cheese, and another flask of wine. Pushing aside the playing cards, he set them all down on the little table. Then he took out a knife from his pocket, a kind of jackknife, which he opened and laid down beside the bread.

'Help yourselves,' he said.

'Could you tell me at least how you found the body?' asked Montalbano, mouth full of bread and cheese.

'No, come on!' Mimì Augello burst out. 'First, he has to finish the game. I haven't won a single one so far!'

*

Mimì lost that one too, and so he wanted another rematch, and another rematch after that. Montalbano, Fazio, and Catarella, who was drying himself by the fire, devoured the tumazzo, which was so tender it melted in one's mouth, and knocked back the entire flask of wine.

Thus an hour passed.

And, as Ajena had predicted, there was a break in the clouds.

TWO

'What the . . . ?' said Ajena, looking down. 'It was right here!'

They stood in a row, elbow to elbow, on a narrow footpath, looking down at a very steep stretch of earth, practically a sheer drop. But it wasn't actually earth, properly speaking. It was an assortment of greyish, yellowish slabs of clay that the rain did not penetrate, all of them covered, or rather coated with a sort of treacherous shaving cream. You could tell from the look of them that you had only to set your foot on them to suddenly find yourself twenty yards below.

'It was right here!' Ajena repeated.

And now it was gone. The travelling corpse, the wandering cadaver.

During the descent towards the spot where Ajena had seen the corpse, it was impossible to exchange so much as a word, because they had to walk in single file, with Ajena at the head, leaning on a shepherd's crook,

17

Montalbano behind, leaning on Ajena, hand on his shoulder, Augello next, hand on Montalbano's shoulder, and Fazio behind him, hand on Augello's shoulder.

Montalbano recalled having seen something similar in a famous painting. Brueghel? Bosch? But this was hardly the moment to think about art.

Catarella, who was the last in line, and not only in a hierarchical sense, didn't have the courage to lean on the shoulder of the person in front of him, and thus slid from time to time in the mud, knocking into Fazio, who knocked into Augello, who knocked into Montalbano, who knocked into Ajena, threatening to bring them all down like ninepins.

'Listen, Ajena,' Montalbano said irritably, 'are you sure this is the right place?'

'Inspector, this land is all mine and I come here every day, rain or shine.'

'Can we talk?'

'If you wanna talk, sir, let's talk,' said Ajena, lighting his pipe.

'So, according to you, the body was here?'

'Wha', you deaf, sir? An' whattya mean, "according to me"? It was right here, I tell you,' said Ajena, gesturing with his pipe at the spot where the slabs of clay began, a short distance from his feet.

'So it was out in the open.'

'Well, yes and no.'

'Explain yourself.'

'Mr Inspector, it's all clay around here. In fact, this place has always been called *'u critaru*, 'n' that's—'

'Why have a place like this?'

'I sell the clay to people who make vases, jugs, pots, that kind of thing . . .'

'All right, go on.'

'Well, when it's not raining, an' it don't rain much around here, today's an exception, but when it don't rain, the clay's all covered up by the earth that slides down the hillside. So you gotta dig down at least a foot to get at it. You follow?'

'Yes.'

'But when it rains, and rains hard, the water washes away the earth on top, an' so the clay comes out. An' that's wha' happened this morning: the rain carried the soil further down an' uncovered the dead body.'

'So you're telling me the body was buried under the earth, and the rain unearthed it?'

'Yessir, that's azackly what I'm saying. I was passing by here on my way up to the cave an' that's when I saw the bag.'

'What bag?'

'A great big plastic bag, black, the kind you use for rubbish.'

'How did you see what was inside? Did you open it?'

'Nah, I didn't need to. The bag had a small hole an' a foot was sticking out, except that all its toes was cut off an' so I couldn't really tell at first if it was a foot.'

'Cut off, you say?'

'Cut off, or maybe et off by a dog.'

'I see. What did you do then?'

'I kept on walking up to the cave.'

'And how did you call the police station?' asked Fazio.

'Wit' my mobile phone, which I keep in my pocket.'

'What time was it when you spotted the bag?' Augello cut in.

'Maybe six in the morning.'

'And it took you over an hour to get from here to the cave and call us?' Augello pressed him.

'And what's it to you, may I ask, how long it took me to call?'

'I'll show you what it is to me!' said Mimì, enraged.

'We got your call at seven-twenty,' Fazio said to the man, trying to explain. 'One hour and twenty minutes after you discovered the bag with the body.'

'What did you do? Make sure to tell someone to come and pick up the body?' Augello asked, suddenly seeming like the dastardly, wicked detective of American movies.

Worried, Montalbano realized Mimì wasn't pretending.

'Whoever said that? What are you thinking? I didn't tell nobody!'

'Then tell us what you did for that hour and twenty minutes.'

Mimì had fastened onto him like a rabid dog and wouldn't let go.

'I was thinking things over.'

'And it took you almost an hour and a half to think things over?'

'Yessirree.'

'To think what over?'

'Whether it was best to phone or not.'

'Why?'

''Cause any time anybody's got to deal with you cops, they end up wishin' they hadn't.'

'Oh, yeah?' said Mimì, turning red in the face and raising his hand to deliver a punch.

'Calm down, Mimì!' said Montalbano.

'Listen,' Augello continued, looking for an excuse to have it out with the man, 'there are two ways to reach the cave, one from above, the other from below. Right?'

'That's right.'

'Why did you take us on the downhill path? So we could break our necks?'

'Because you would never make it uphill. With all this rain the path's slippery as hell.'

They heard a dull rumble, and all looked up at the sky. The break in the clouds was beginning to close. They all were thinking the same thing: if they didn't find that body soon, they were going to get even more soaked.

'How do you explain the fact that the body is gone?' Montalbano intervened.

'Well,' said Ajena, 'either the body got flushed down to the bottom by the water and soil, or somebody came and took it.'

'Go on!' said Mimì. 'If somebody came and took the bag, they would've left a trail in the mud! Whereas there's nothing!'

'Whattya mean, sir?' Ajena retorted. 'Do you really think after all this rain you're still gonna see tracks?'

At this point in the discussion, for who knows what reason, Catarella took a step forward. And thus began his second slide of the morning. He had only to set one foot half down on the clay to execute a figure-skating sort of split, one foot on the path, the other on the edge of a clay slab. Fazio, who was standing beside him, tried to grab him, to no avail. In fact, he only managed to give him a strong if involuntary push. Thus in a split-second Catarella spread his arms, then spun around, turning his back as his legs flew out from under him.

'I loss my balaaaa . . .' he announced loudly to one and all as he fell down hard and as though sitting on an invisible sled began to gain momentum (reminding Montalbano of a law of physics he had learned at school: *Motus in fine velocior*), whereupon he fell head-backwards, shoulders to the mud, and careered downwards with the speed of a bobsleigher. His race ended some twenty yards below, at the bottom of the slope, in a large bush which Catarella's body entered like a bullet and disappeared into.

*

None of the spectators uttered a word; none made a move. They just stood there, spellbound.

'Get that man some first aid,' Montalbano ordered after a moment.

He was so severely annoyed by the whole affair that he didn't even feel like laughing.

'How do we get down there to pull him out?' Augello asked Ajena.

'If we go down this same footpath we'll come to a spot not far from where the p'liceman ended up.'

'Then let's get moving.'

But at that moment Catarella emerged from the bush. He'd lost his trousers and pants in the slide and was prudishly holding his hands over his private parts.

'Did you hurt yourself?' Fazio shouted.

'Nah. But I found the body bag. Iss here.'

'Should we go down there?' Mimì Augello asked Montalbano.

'No. Now we know where it is. Fazio, you go down and get Catarella. You, Mimì, go and wait for them in the cave.'

'And what about you?' asked Augello.

'I'm going to get in the Jeep and go home. I've had enough of this.'

'I beg your pardon? What about the investigation?'

'What investigation, Mimì? If the body was fresh, then our presence here might serve some purpose. But who knows when and where this person was murdered? You need to call the prosecutor, the coroner, and the forensics lab. Do it now, Mimì.'

'But to get here from Montelusa, it'll take them a good two hours at the very least!'

'In two hours it'll be raining hard again,' Ajena chimed in.

'So much the better,' said Montalbano. 'Why should we be the only ones to get soaked to the bone?'

'And what am I supposed to do for two hours?' Mimì asked sullenly.

'You can play cards,' said the inspector. Then, seeing Ajena walking away, he added: 'Why did you call Catarella and tell him my presence was indispensable here?'

'Because I thought that—'

'Mimì, you didn't think anything. You wanted to make me come here for the sole purpose of annoying me, getting me drenched like everybody else.'

'Salvo, you just said it yourself: Why should only Fazio and I get soaked while you're still lying in bed?'

Montalbano couldn't help but notice how much anger there was in Augello's words. He hadn't done it as a joke. What on earth was happening to him?

*

When he got back to Marinella it had already started pouring again. It was well past lunchtime, and spending the morning in the open air had whetted his appetite. He went into the bathroom, changed out of his rain-soaked suit, and hurried into the kitchen. Adelina had made him pasta *'ncasciata* and, as a second course, rabbit *alla cacciatore*. She very rarely made this, but whenever she did, it brought tears of happiness to his eyes.

*

By the time Fazio straggled back into the station, night was falling. He must have gone home first, showered and changed, but he was visibly tired. It hadn't been an easy day at *'u critaru*.

'Where's Mimì?'

'Gone home to rest, Chief. He felt a bit of fever coming on.'

'And Catarella?'

'Him too. Over a hundred, I'd say. He wanted to come in anyway, but I told him to go home and lie down.'

'Did you recover the bag with the body?'

'You know what, Chief? When we went back to *'u critaru* in the pouring rain with the forensics team, the prosecutor, Dr Pasquano, and the stretcher-bearers, and we looked in the bushes where Catarella said he saw the bag, it was gone!'

'Jesus Christ, what a pain in the arse! The corpse that wouldn't stay put! So where was it?'

'The water and sludge had carried it about ten yards further down. But part of the bag got torn, so a few of the pieces—'

'Pieces? What pieces?'

'Before the body was put in the bag, it had been cut into small pieces.'

So Ajena was right about what he'd seen: the toes had been cut off the feet.

'So what did you do?'

'We had to wait till Cocò arrived from Montelusa.'

'And who's Cocò? Never heard of him.'

'Cocò's a dog, Chief. A really good dog. He found five body parts that had fallen out of the bag and got scattered about, including the head. After which Dr Pasquano said that as far as he could tell, the corpse seemed complete. And so we were finally able to leave.'

'Did you see the head yourself?'

'I did, but you couldn't tell anything from it. The face was gone. It'd been totally obliterated by repeated blows from a hammer or mallet, or some heavy object.'

'They didn't want him recognized right away.'

'No doubt about it, Chief. 'Cause I also saw the index finger of the right hand, which had been cut off. The whole fingertip had been burned off.'

'You know what that means, don't you?'

'Of course, Chief. That the victim had a record and could have been identified from his fingerprints. So they took the necessary measures.'

'Was Pasquano able to determine how long ago he was killed?'

'He said two months, at the very least. But he needs to have a better look at him in the post-mortem.'

'Do you know when he'll do that?'

'Tomorrow morning.'

'And there was no report of this man's disappearance over those two months?'

'There are two possibilities, Chief: either it wasn't reported, or it was.'

Montalbano gave him a look of mock admiration.

'Well done, Fazio! Ever heard of Monsieur de la Palisse?'

'No, Chief. Who was he?'

'A man who fifteen minutes before he died was still alive.'

Fazio immediately got it.

'Come on, Chief! You didn't let me finish my thought!'

'All right then, go on. For a brief moment I thought you'd been infected by Catarella.'

'What I meant was that it's possible somebody reported the dead man's disappearance, but since we don't know who the dead man is—'

'I get your point. The only thing we can do is wait till tomorrow to see what Pasquano has to tell us.'

*

Once home, he was greeted by the telephone, which started ringing as he was trying to unlock the door, fumbling with the keys.

'Hello, darling, how are you?'

It was Livia, sounding cheerful.

'I had a pretty rough morning. How about you?'

'I've been great, for my part. I didn't go to the office today.'

'Oh, really? Why not?'

'I didn't feel like it. It was such a beautiful morning. It seemed like a terrible shame to go to work. You should have seen the sun, Salvo. It looked like yours.'

'So what did you do?'

'I went out and had fun.'

'Well, you can afford to.'

It had slipped out, and Livia didn't let it slide.

*

A little while later, still in a bad mood, he settled down to watch television. On a chair beside his armchair he had put two dishes, one full of green and black olives and salted sardines, the other with cheese, tumazzo and caciocavallo di Ragusa. He poured himself a glass of wine but kept the bottle within reach, just in case. Then he turned on the TV. The first thing that came on was a film set in some Asian country during the monsoon. What? It's a deluge outside and now he has to watch a fake deluge on TV? He changed the channel. Another movie. A woman lay naked on a bed, batting her eyelashes at a young man undressing and seen from behind. When he took off his pants, the woman's eyes opened wide and she brought a hand to her mouth, surprised and amazed by what she saw. He changed the channel. The Prime Minister was explaining why the country's economy was going to the dogs: the first reason was the terrorist attack on the Twin Towers; the second was the tsunami in the Pacific; the third was the euro; the fourth the Communist opposition that refused to cooperate, and ... He changed the channel. There was a cardinal talking about the sacred institution of the family. In the first row of the audience were an array of politicians, two of whom were divorced, another who was living with a minor after leaving his wife and three children, a fourth who maintained an official family and two unofficial families, and a fifth who had never married because, as was well known, he didn't like women. All nodded gravely in agreement with the cardinal's words. He changed the channel. The screen filled with the chicken-arse face of Pippo Ragonese, the top newsman of TeleVigàta.

'. . . and so the discovery of the corpse of a man brutally murdered, cut into small pieces, and put into a rubbish bag, disturbs us for several reasons. But the principal one is that the investigation has been assigned to Chief Inspector Salvo Montalbano of the Vigàta Police, on whom we have, unfortunately, had occasion to focus our attention in the past. Our criticisms were directed not so much at the fact that he has political ideas — indeed every word he says is steeped in Communist beliefs — but at the fact that he has no ideas at all during his investigations. Or else, when he does, they are always absurd, outlandish, and utterly groundless. So we would like to give him some advice. But will he listen? The advice is the following. Only two weeks ago, in the area around the place called 'u critaru, where the corpse was found, a hunter ran across two plastic bags containing the remains of two suckling calves. Might there not be a connection between these two occurrences? Might it not involve some satanic rite that—'

He turned off the TV. Satanic rite, my arse! Aside from the fact that the two bags had been found two and a half miles away from 'u critaru, it was discovered that they'd been dumped following an operation by the carabinieri to stop unauthorized animal slaughter.

He went to bed feeling fed up with all of creation. But before lying down he took an aspirin, cursing the saints all the while. Given the soaking he'd endured that morning and his wretchedly advancing age, perhaps it was best to be cautious.

*

The following morning, after awaking from a night of somewhat agitated sleep and opening the window, the inspector rejoiced. The sun shone as bright as July in a sky scrubbed perfectly clean and sparkling. The sea, which for two days had completely covered the beach, had withdrawn, but had left the sand littered with rubbish bags, empty cans, plastic bottles, bottomless boxes and various other filth. Montalbano recalled how in now distant times, when the sea withdrew, it would leave behind only sweet-smelling algae and beautiful shells that were like gifts to mankind. Now it only gave back our own rubbish.

He also remembered a comedy he had read in his youth, called *The Deluge*, which claimed that the next great flood would be caused not by water from the heavens, but by the backing up and overflowing of all the toilets, latrines, cesspools and septic tanks in the world, which would start chucking up their contents relentlessly until we all drowned in our own shit.

He went out on the veranda and stepped down onto the beach.

He noticed that the space between the cement slab holding up the veranda's tiled floor and the sand below had become clogged with a fine assortment of stinking debris, including the carcass of a dog.

Cursing like a madman, he went back inside, slipped on a pair of dishwashing gloves, grabbed a sort of hook or grapnel that Adelina used for mysterious purposes, went down to the beach again, threw himself down on the sand and started cleaning up.

After fifteen minutes of this, a sharp pang seized him across the shoulders, paralysing him. Why on earth was he undertaking such tasks at his age?

Can I really be in such bad shape? he wondered.

In a fit of pride, however, he went back to work, the pain be damned. When he had finished putting all the rubbish into two large bags, every bone in his body ached. But he'd had an idea in the meantime, and he had to see it through. He went inside and wrote in block letters on a blank sheet of paper: SHIT. He put this in one of the two bags, which he then picked up and put into the boot of his car. He went back into the house, showered, dressed, got into his car, and drove off.

THREE

Just outside a town called Rattusa, he spotted a telephone booth that miraculously worked. He pulled up, got out of the car, and dialled a number.

'Is this Pippo Ragonese, the newsman?'

'In person. Who is this?'

'The name's Russo, Luicino Russo. I'm a hunter,' said Montalbano, changing his voice.

'What can I do for you, Mr Russo?'

'Iss happened again,' said the inspector in a conspiratorial tone of voice.

'I'm sorry, what's happened again?'

'That satanic stuff you talked about lass night on TV. I foun' two more bags.'

'Really?' asked Ragonese, immediately interested. 'Where did you find them?'

'Right here,' said Montalbano, playing dumb.

'Here where?'

'Right here where I am.'

'Yes, but where are you?'

'In Spiranzella district, right by the four big olive trees.'

That is, about thirty miles from the newsman's house.

'Wha' should I do? Call the police?' asked Montalbano.

'No, there's no need, we can do that together. You stay put for the moment. I'll be there straight away. And don't tell anyone else, please, it's very important.'

'You comin' alone?'

'No, I'll bring a cameraman as well.'

'Will he take me?'

'What do you mean?'

'Will he take my pitcher? Will I be on TV? So all my friends'll see me an' I can boast about it?'

He got back into the car, drove to Spiranzella, left the two bags under one of the four olive trees, and drove off.

*

Entering the station, he found Catarella at his post.

'But didn't you have a fever?'

'I got rid of it, Chief.'

'How'd you do that?'

'Took four aspirins an' then drunk a glass o' hot spicy wine an' then got in bed an' covered m'self up. An' now iss gone.'

'Who's here?'

'Fazio in't here yet, an' Isspector Augello called sayin' as how he still had a little fever but would come in later in the morning.'

'Any news?'

'There's a ginnelman wants a talk to yiz whose name is – wait, I got it writ down somewheres – iss an easy name but I forgot it, wait, here it is: Giacchetta.'

'Does that seem like a forgettable name to you?'

'It happens to me sometimes, Chief.'

'All right, then, send him into my office after I go in.'

*

The man who came in was well dressed, about forty, with a distinguished air, perfectly coiffed hair, moustache, spectacles, and the overall look of an ideal bank clerk.

'Please sit down, Mr Giacchetta.'

'Giacchetti. Fabio Giacchetti's the name.'

Montalbano cursed to himself. Why did he still believe the names Catarella passed on to him?

'What can I do for you, Mr Giacchetti?'

The man sat down, carefully arranging the creases in his trousers and smoothing his moustache. He leaned back in his chair and looked at the inspector.

'Well?' said Montalbano.

'The truth of the matter is, I'm not sure I was right to come here.'

O matre santa! He'd happened upon a ditherer, a doubting Thomas, the worst kind of person who might ever walk into a police station.

'Listen, I can't help you with that. It's up to you to decide. It's not like I can give you little hints the way they do on game shows.'

'Well, the fact is that last night I witnessed something . . . and that's just it, I don't know what it was . . . something I really don't know how to define.'

'If you decide to tell me what it was, perhaps together we can arrive at a definition,' said Montalbano, who was beginning to feel irritated. 'If, on the other hand, you don't tell me, then I'll have to send you on your way.'

'Well, at the time, it seemed to me . . . at first, that is, it looked to me like a hit-and-run driver. You know what I mean, don't you?'

'Yes. Or at least I can tell a hit-and-run driver from a hit-and-run lover — you know, the kind with bedroom eyes and a little black book. Listen, Mr Giacchetti, I haven't got much time to waste. Let's start at the beginning, all right? I'll ask you a few questions, just to warm you up, so to speak.'

'OK.'

'Are you from here?'

'No, I'm from Rome.'

'And what do you do here in Vigàta?'

'I started three months ago as manager of the branch office of the Banco Cooperativo.'

The inspector had been right. The man could only be with a bank. You can tell right away: those who handle other people's money in the cathedrals of wealth that are the big banks end up acquiring something austere and reserved in their manner, something priestlike proper to those who practise secret rites such as laundering dirty money, engaging in legalized usury, using coded accounts, and illegally exporting capital. They suffer, in short, from the same sort of occupational deformities as undertakers, who, in handling corpses every day, end up looking like walking corpses themselves.

'Where do you live?'

'For now, while waiting to find a decent apartment, my wife and I are staying at a house on the Montereale road, as her parents' guests. It's their country home, but they've lent it to us for the time being.'

'All right, then, if you'd be so kind as to tell me what happened...'

'Last night, around 2 a.m., my wife started going into labour, and so I put her in the car and we headed off to Montelusa Hospital.'

The man was finally opening up.

'Just as we were leaving Vigàta, I noticed, in the headlights, a woman walking ahead of me, with her back to me. At that moment a car came up beside me at high speed, lightly swiping my car as it passed – it looked to me like it was swerving – and then it aimed straight for the woman. She quickly realized the danger, probably hearing the engine, jumped to her right and fell into the ditch. The car stopped for a second and then screeched off again.'

'So it didn't hit her?'

'No. She dodged it.'

'And what did you do?'

'I stopped, though my wife was crying – she was feeling very bad by this point – and I got out. The woman had got up in the meantime. I asked her if she was hurt and she said no. So I told her to get in the car and I would take her into town, and she accepted. On the way, we all agreed that the driver must have had a bit too much to drink, and that it must have been some sort of stupid joke. Then she told me where she wanted to be dropped off, and she got out of the car. Before she left, however, she begged me not to tell anyone about what I had seen. She gave me to understand that she was returning from an amorous encounter...'

'She didn't explain how she happened to be out alone at that hour of the night?'

'She made some reference . . . she said her car had stalled and wouldn't start up again. But then she realized she had run out of petrol.'

'So how did things work out?'

Fabio Giacchetti looked confused.

'With the lady?'

'No, with your wife.'

'I don't ... I don't understand...'

'Did you become a father or not?'

Fabio Giacchetti lit up.

'Yes. A boy.'

'Congratulations. Tell me something: how old do you think the woman was?'

Fabio Giacchetti smiled.

'About thirty, Inspector. Tall, dark, and very attractive. Clearly upset, but very attractive.'

'Where did she get out?'

'At the corner of Via Serpotta and Via Guttuso.'

'So you've learned the names of all the streets in Vigàta after only three months?'

Fabio Giacchetti blushed.

'No ... it's just that ... when the lady got out ... I looked at the names of the streets.'

'Why?'

Fabio Giacchetti blazed red.

'Well, you know ... instinctively ...'

Instinctively indeed! Fabio Giacchetti had looked for the street names because the woman appealed to him and he would like to meet her again. A devoted husband, happy father, and potential adulterer.

'Listen, Mr Giacchetti, you told me that at first you thought it might be a hit-and-run incident, and then, after talking to the woman, you both agreed that it was some sort of dangerous, stupid joke. And now you're here, talking to me. Why? Did you change your mind again?'

Fabio Giacchetti hesitated.

'Well, it's not that I ... but there *is* something ...'

'Something that doesn't make sense to you?'

'Well, you see, when I was at the hospital, waiting for Elena to give birth, I thought again about what had happened ... Not for any particular reason, but just to distract myself ... When the car that had aimed at the woman stopped, I instinctively slowed down ... and at that moment, it looked to me as if the man at the wheel leaned out of the window on the passenger's side and said something to the woman in the ditch ... Whereas, logically speaking, he should have driven away in a hurry ... He was taking a huge risk ... I could read his licence plate, for example ...'

'Did you?'

'Yes, but then I forgot it. It began with CE. Perhaps if I ever saw the car again . . . And then I had the impression, but I don't know whether ...'

'Tell me.'

'I had the impression the woman talked to me about what had just happened only because I had witnessed it and started talking about it myself. I don't know if I've made myself clear.'

'You've made yourself perfectly clear. The woman had no desire to go over the incident.'

'Precisely, Inspector.'

'One last question. You got the impression that the

man at the wheel said something to the woman . . . Could you better explain why you had this impression?'

'Because I saw his head poke out of the passenger-side window.'

'Couldn't he perhaps have stopped only to see what sort of condition the woman was in?'

'I would rule that out. The more I think about it, the more convinced I am that he said something to her. You see, he made a gesture with his hand, as if to emphasize what he was saying.'

'What kind of gesture?'

'I didn't get a good look; but I did see his hand outside the window, that much I know.'

'But the woman didn't tell you he had said anything to her.'

'No.'

*

He repeated to Fazio, who turned up late that morning, the story Giacchetti had told him.

'Chief, what can we do about it if some drunk behind the wheel gets his kicks from scaring a lady by pretending to run her over?'

'So you're of the opinion that it was a bad joke? Mind you, that's also the interpretation the beautiful stranger tried to convince the banker of.'

'You don't agree?'

'Let me speculate a little. Couldn't it have been attempted murder?'

Fazio looked doubtful.

'In the presence of witnesses, Chief? Giacchetti was right behind him.'

'Excuse me, Fazio, but if he'd killed her, what could Giacchetti have done?'

'Well, for starters, he could have taken down the licence number.'

'And what if it was a stolen car?'

Fazio didn't answer.

'No, this whole thing stinks to me,' Montalbano continued.

'But why?'

'Because he didn't kill her, Fazio. Because he only wanted to scare her. And not as a joke. He stopped, said something to the woman, and then left. And the woman did everything possible to downplay the matter.'

'Listen, Chief, if it's the way you say it is, couldn't the person in the car have been, I dunno, a jilted lover or suitor?'

'Maybe. And that's what worries me. He might try again and seriously injure or kill her.'

'You want me to look into it?'

'Yes, but don't waste too much time on it. The whole thing might turn out to be nothing.'

'Where did this lady ask to be dropped off?'

'At the corner of Via Serpotta and Via Guttuso.'

Fazio winced.

'What's wrong? Don't you like Guttuso?'

'I don't like that neighbourhood, Chief. That's where the rich people live.'

'Don't you like rich people? What is this, anyway? You used to accuse me of being an angry Communist, and now you—'

'Communism's got nothing to do with it, Chief. The fact is that rich people are always a pain in the arse. They're hard to deal with; you say one word too many and they clam up.'

*

'Ah, Chief, the Signorina Zita's onna line an' wants a talk to yiz poissonally in poisson.'

'And who's this Zita?'

'You kiddin' me, Chief?'

'No, Cat, I'm not. I don't feel like talking to her.'

'You sure, Chief?'

'I'm sure.'

'Want me to tell 'er yer not onna premisses?'

'Tell her whatever the hell you want.'

*

Shortly before the inspector decided it was time to eat, Mimì Augello came in. He looked fairly well rested. But he was gloomy.

'How are you feeling, Mimì?'

43

'I've still got a bit of fever, but I feel well enough to be up. I wanted to know what you intend to do.'

'About what?'

'Salvo, don't pretend you don't understand. I'm referring to the body in the bag. Let's make things perfectly clear; that way there won't be any misunderstandings or mistakes. Are you going to handle the case, or am I?'

'Sorry, but I really don't understand. Who's the head of this department, you or me?'

'If you put it that way, then it's clear we have nothing to say to each other. The case is yours by rights.'

'Mimì, may I ask what's got into you? Haven't I let you operate with total autonomy lately? Haven't I given you more and more space? What is your complaint?'

'That's true. You used to stick your nose into everything, whereas now you're a little less meddlesome. In fact you often let me do the investigating.'

'So what's the problem?'

'Yes, but investigate what? Basically rubbish. Supermarket burglaries, holdups at the post office . . .'

'And what about the murder of Dr Calì?'

'Come on! We practically caught Mrs Calì with the gun still warm in her hand! Some investigation, that! The present case is different. The body in the bag is one of those challenges that can make you feel like working again.'

'So?'

'I don't want you to give me the case only to take it

away from me later on. I want an explicit agreement, OK?'

'Mimì, I don't like the way you're talking to me.'

'Goodbye, Salvo,' said Augello, turning his back and leaving the room.

What on earth was wrong with Mimì? He'd been in a foul mood for over a month now. Nervous, often silent, always ready to take offence over the slightest remark. At certain moments you could tell he wasn't all there, his mind far away. Clearly something was eating at him. Was this what married life with Beba had come to? And yet at first he had seemed so happy, especially over the birth of his son. Surely Livia could tell him something about this. She and Beba had become very good friends and often talked on the phone.

He left the station and drove off towards Enzo's trattoria. On the way, however, he realized that his talk with Mimì had killed his appetite. It certainly wasn't the first time they'd had an argument, and on a few occasions things had even turned ugly. This time, however, he'd noticed a different tone in Mimì's words. The real purpose of their discussion was not to determine who would handle the investigation. No, the real purpose was something else: Mimì had simply wanted to have it out with him. Just as he'd done with Ajena the day before. He was looking to let off steam. Looking for a pretext to spew out all the black bile he had building up inside him.

When he got home, Montalbano sat down on the veranda and lay like a lizard in the sun.

＊

That afternoon, before returning to the station, he phoned Catarella.

'Has Dr Pasquano called for me?'

'Nossir, Chief.'

He hung up and dialled another number.

'Montalbano here. Is Dr Pasquano there?'

'Well, he's here, Inspector, as far as that goes. But I don't know if he can come to the telephone. He's working.'

'Try.'

While waiting, he revised the times table for seven, which was the hardest for him.

'What a colossal pain in the arse you are, Inspector! What the hell do you want?' Pasquano began, with the gentle courtesy for which he was famous.

'Have you done the post-mortem?'

'Which one? The little girl who had her throat slit? The drowned Moroccan? The peasant who was shot? The—'

'The man found chopped to pieces in a rubbish bag.'

'Yes.'

'Could you—'

'No.'

'What if I came to see you in half an hour?'
'Make that an hour.'

*

When he arrived and asked for Pasquano, an assistant replied that the doctor was still busy and had given instructions to have the inspector wait for him in his office.

The first thing Montalbano noticed on Pasquano's desk, between the papers and photographs of murder victims, was a cardboard pastry-shop tray full of giant cream horns and a bottle of Pantelleria raisin wine and a glass beside it. Pasquano had a notorious sweet tooth. The inspector bent down to smell the cream horns: fresh as could be. So he poured himself a little of the sweet wine into the glass, picked up a cream horn and started eating it while contemplating the landscape through the open window.

The sun lit up the colours in the valley, making them stand out sharply against the blue sea in the distance. God, or whoever was acting in his stead, had assumed the guise of a naïf painter here. On the horizon, a flock of seagulls frolicked about, pretending to squabble among themselves in a parade of nosedives, veers, and pull-ups that looked exactly like an aerobatics show. He watched their manoeuvres, spellbound.

Having finished the first cream horn, he took another.

ANDREA CAMILLERI

'I see you've helped yourself,' said Pasquano, coming
in and grabbing one.

They ate in religious silence, the corners of their
mouths smeared with ricotta cream. Which, the rules say,
must be removed with a slow, circular movement of the
tongue.

FOUR

'So, what can you tell me, Doctor?' the inspector asked after they had drunk some of the sweet wine, passing the only available glass back and forth.

'About what? The international situation? My haemorrhoids?'

'About the body in the bag.'

'Oh, that? It was a long and aggravating process. First I had to complete the puzzle.'

'The puzzle?'

'I had to piece the body back together, my friend. It had been dismembered, remember?'

'I do,' Montalbano replied, grinning.

'You find that amusing?'

'No, I find the verb you use amusing.'

'Dismember? You don't like the rhyme with "remember"? *Try to remember the man you dismembered . . .*,' the doctor sang. 'If you prefer, I could use some other verb, like dice, quarter, butcher . . .'

'Let's just say "chopped up". Into how many pieces?'

'Quite a few. They spared no effort in their butchery. They used a hatchet and a large, very sharp cleaver. First they killed him, and then—'

'How?'

'A single gunshot at the base of the skull.'

'When?'

'Let's say two months ago, maximum. Then, as I was saying, they burned off his fingertips. After which they got down to work. With saintly patience they cut off all his fingers and toes and both ears, then smashed up his face until it was unrecognizable, pulled out all his teeth, which we were unable to find, chopped off his head, hands, both legs all the way up to the groin, the right arm and forearm, but only the left forearm. Strange, isn't it?'

'All this butchery, you mean?'

'No, the fact that they left the left upper arm. I wonder why they didn't cut that off, too, while they were at it?'

'Have you found anything that might lead to a quick identification?'

'Not a fucking thing.'

'Speaking of which, Doctor: and the sex organ?'

'Not doing too badly, thank you very much. Nothing to worry about.'

'No, Doctor, what I mean is: did they cut off his sex organ as well?'

'If they had, I would have mentioned it.'

'How old was he?'

'About forty.'

'Height?'

'Not less than five foot ten.'

'Non-European?'

'Hardly! One of ours.'

'Fat? Thin?'

'Trim and in excellent shape.'

'Can you tell me anything else?'

'Yes. When he was killed, he hadn't yet evacuated.'

'Is that important?'

'It certainly is. Because we found something of possible importance in his stomach.'

'Namely?'

'He'd swallowed a bridge.'

Montalbano balked.

'What kind of bridge?'

'The Brooklyn Bridge.'

'What?'

'Has the wine gone to your head, Montalbano? I'm talking about teeth. The bridge may have come loose while he was eating, and he may have swallowed it later by accident.'

The inspector thought about this a moment.

'Couldn't the bridge have ended up in his stomach while they were mangling his face?'

'No, it would have remained in his mouth or throat.

The body can't swallow after it's dead. He may have swallowed it during some trauma before he was shot.'

'What did you do with it?'

'I sent it immediately to Forensics. You realize, however, that it'll be months before they can tell us anything about it.'

'Right,' said Montalbano, discouraged.

'And don't expect them to be able to tell you the name of the victim's dentist, either.'

'Right,' Montalbano repeated, more disconsolate than ever.

'Want another cream horn?'

'No. Thanks anyway. I'll be seeing you.'

'You will? I hope not to see you again for a good while,' said the doctor, sinking his teeth into a second cream horn himself.

*

But Pasquano had told him something of great importance. The man had been killed by a gunshot at the base of the skull. Execution-style. With hands and feet bound, the poor bastard had been forced to kneel, and the executioner had fired a single shot into his brain.

It was as if the Mafia had actually left its signature.

But questions still remained. All of them. Who was he? Why was he killed? Why go to such trouble to make him unrecognizable? Why cut him into so many pieces? Certainly not to facilitate moving the body. There are other ways to do that. Like dissolving the body in acid. And why did they bury the body at 'u critaru under a foot of topsoil? Didn't they know that with the first heavy rains the bag would be unearthed? There was a rocky crag barely fifty yards further up: under a pile of rocks the bag would never have been found.

No, it was clear that the killers wanted the body to be discovered, after a certain amount of time had passed.

*

'Ah, Chief, Chief! Fazio tol' me a tell yiz 'at the minute y'got back I's asposta tell 'im y'got back.'

'All right, then tell him and send him to my office.'

Fazio arrived at once.

'Before you say anything, let me talk first. I've been to see Pasquano.'

And he told him what the doctor had said.

'So, in conclusion,' said Fazio, 'the victim was a forty-year-old man, five feet ten inches tall, and trim. Not much to get excited about. I'll start looking into the missing-persons reports.'

'Meanwhile tell me what you wanted to tell me.'

'Chief, the woman you wanted information on is called Dolores Alfano. She's thirty-one, married without children, and lives at Via Guttoso 12. She's foreign, maybe Spanish. Alfano met her abroad when she was twenty, fell head over heels for her and married her. And she is, in fact, a very beautiful woman.'

'Have you seen her?'

'No, but every single man I talked to raved about her looks.'

'Does she have a car?'

'Yes. A Fiat Punto.'

'What does she do?'

'Nothing. Housewife.'

'What about the husband?'

'Sea captain. At the moment he's sailing as a first mate on a container ship. He's been out of the country for the past few months. They say if the husband comes home four times a year it's a lot.'

'So, in theory, the poor girl is forced to go hungry. Did you hear anything to the contrary? Did anyone suggest that she fools around when the husband's away?'

'I got some conflicting reports. For one or two people, Signora Dolores is a slut who's too shrewd to get caught in the act; for others she's a woman who is so beautiful that if she does have a lover, she's right to have one, since her husband is always away; for the majority, however, she's a virtuous woman.'

'Sounds like you held a referendum!'

'But, Chief, men just love to talk about a woman like that!'

'In essence, though, it's all smoke and no fire. All gossip. You know what I say? Let's forget about her. Maybe the attempt to run her over really was nothing more than a moronic joke.'

'On the other hand...' said Fazio.

'On the other hand?'

'If you'll allow me, I'd like to try to find out more about this woman.'

'Why?'

'At the moment I can't really explain it, Chief. But there's something somebody said to me that made me wonder. It was sort of a flash, an idea, that immediately faded. I don't remember if it was a single word or a phrase, or if it was the way the word or phrase was said to me. Or maybe it was just a silent stare that seemed important to me at that moment.'

'You don't remember who the person was at all?'

'I'm having trouble bringing it into focus, Chief. I talked to about ten people in all, women as well as men. I can't very well go back and ask them the same questions.'

'Do what you think best.'

*

Phoning Vanni Arquà, the chief of the Forensics Laboratory, was always a pain. The inspector didn't like him one bit, and the feeling was amply returned in kind.

But he had no choice. Because if he didn't call him himself, Arquà would never relay any information to him. Before picking up the receiver, Montalbano took a deep breath, as if about to plunge underwater, all the while repeating to himself:

Easy does it, Salvo, easy...

He dialled the number.

'Arquà? Montalbano here.'

'What do you want? Look, I haven't got any time to waste.'

To avoid blowing up right off the bat, he clenched his teeth so hard that the words came out very strangely.

'I hrd tht ths mrning—'

'Why are you talking that way?'

'What way? I'm talking the way I always talk. I heard that this morning Dr Pasquano sent you a bridge he'd found—'

'Yes, he did. So what? Goodbye.'

'No, I'm sorry . . . but, if possible, I would like . . . a little more quickly . . . I realize how swamped with work you people are . . . but you must realize that . . . for me . . .'

In the effort to try to be nice, to avoid hurling abuse at Arquà, he became incapable of constructing a complete sentence. He felt furious at himself.

'The bridge is no longer here with us.'

'Where is it?'

'We sent it to Palermo, to Professor Lomascolo's lab.'

Arquà hung up. Montalbano carefully wiped away the sweat that was drenching his brow and redialled the number.

'Arquà? Montalbano again. I'm truly sorry to bother you again.'

'Speak.'

'If I may, I forgot something important.'

'What did you forget?'

'To tell you to go and fuck yourself.'

He hung up. If he hadn't got it out of his system, he would have been on edge for the rest of the evening. All in all, however, the fact that the bridge was in the hands of Professor Lomascolo was good news. The professor was a real authority and would surely be able to glean some information from it. And, moreover, the inspector had always got on well with him. But it was clear by now that if by some stroke of luck this case ever managed to move ahead, it would move very slowly.

*

Back in Marinella, he dawdled about the house for an hour or so. Before sitting down in front of the television he decided to call Livia and apologize for the quarrel of the previous night.

'Ah, at last the great Montalbano deigns to grand me an audience!' Livia said angrily.

A joyous start is the best of guides, as Matteo Maria Boiardo famously said.

If this was Livia's tone starting out, how would the phone call end? With an exchange of nuclear missiles? And how should he proceed now? With a nasty retort? No, it was better to take the temperature down a few degrees and find out why she was so upset.

'Darling, you've got to believe me, I wasn't able to call you any sooner because—'

'But it was *I* who called *you*, and you refused to talk to me! God Almighty in heaven can't find a minute to talk to me!'

Montalbano balked.

'You called me? When?'

'This morning, at your office.'

'Maybe they didn't put the call through to me . . .'

'But they did! They most certainly did!'

'Are you sure?'

'I talked to Catarella and he told me you were busy and couldn't pick up.'

He suddenly remembered that Catarella had told him there was a 'Signorina Zita' on the line . . .

'Livia, it was a simple misunderstanding! Catarella didn't make it clear to me that it was you. He only said there was a "Signorina Zita" – "zita", you see, means "girlfriend" to us, but it's also a common surname around here! And since I didn't know any young women by the name of Zita—'

'Let's just forget about it.'

'Livia, try to understand. It was a simple mistake, I tell you! On top of that, you never call me at the office. What did you want to tell me?'

'I wanted you to call me tonight, because I have something important to talk to you about.'

'Well, isn't that what I did? I called you on my own initiative. What's this important thing, then?'

'This morning, before leaving for work, I got a very long phone call from Beba. She's mad at you.'

'Beba? Mad at me? Why?'

'She says you've been treating Mimì very badly.'

'And what on earth has Augello been telling Beba?'

'Are you saying it's not true?'

'Well, it's true that lately he's become very irritable and we've had a few arguments, but nothing serious ... Treating him badly! He's the one who's become impossible to deal with, and in fact I had planned to ask you if by any chance Beba had mentioned anything to you about all this irritability on Mimì's part.'

'So you don't know why he's so irritable?'

'I assure you I don't.'

'Have you forgotten all the times you've sent him on stake-outs in the middle of the night over the past month? And which you continue to do practically every other night?'

Montalbano remained silent, mouth agape.

What the hell was Livia talking about? Was she simply babbling?

Over the past month they had done only one night-time stake-out, and Fazio had handled it alone.

'Aren't you going to say anything?'

'Well, it's just that ...'

'Then I'll go on. The other evening, for example, Mimì came home with a touch of fever after having spent the whole day in the rain to recover a dead body in a bag … Is that true or not?'

'Yes, that's true.'

'Then, just after he had finished eating dinner and wanted to go to bed, you phoned him and forced him to get dressed again and spend the night outside. Don't you think you're being a little sadistic?'

What was going on? Why was Mimì telling Beba all these lies? Whatever the case, it was probably best, for the time being, to let Livia believe that what Mimì said was true.

'Well, I guess … but it's not sadism, Livia. The fact is that I have so few men that I can really trust . . . At any rate, try to reassure Beba. Tell her just to be patient for a little while longer, and that once I get some new personnel, I won't take advantage of Mimì any more.'

'Is that a promise?'

'Absolutely.'

This time the phone call didn't end in a quarrel. Because no matter what Livia said, he always agreed, like an automaton.

*

After talking to Livia, he felt so weak he couldn't move. He remained standing beside the little table, receiver in hand. Numb. Embalmed. Then, dragging his feet, he went and sat down on the veranda. Unfortunately there was only one possible explanation for Mimì's lies. Because it was well known that Mimì didn't drink, didn't gamble, didn't run with the wrong crowd. He had only one vice, if it was indeed a vice. Surely, after almost two years of marriage, Mimì had grown tired of going to bed every night with the same woman and had resumed his wandering ways. Before marrying Beba, his life was a continually revolving door of women, and apparently he had gone back to his old habits. The excuse he gave to his wife so that he could spend nights away from home was perfect. He hadn't foreseen, however, that Beba would talk about it with Livia and that Livia would talk about it in turn with his superior. But one question remained. Why indeed was Mimì so irritable? Why was he so at odds with everyone? It used to be that after he had been with a woman he would show up at work purring like a cat after a good meal. This new relationship must therefore be a burden on him. He wasn't taking it lightly. Perhaps because, before, he didn't have to answer to anybody, whereas now, when he went home, he was forced to lie to Beba, to deceive her. He must be feeling something that had never even crossed his mind before: a strong sense of guilt.

In conclusion, he, Montalbano, had to intervene, even if it was the last thing he felt like doing. There was no getting around it; he had to, like it or not. If he didn't, Mimì would keep staying out at night, saying it was by order of his boss, Beba would complain again to Livia, and this would mean trouble for all eternity. He had to step in, more for his own peace of mind than for that of Mimì and his family.

But intervene how?

That was the rub. A heart-to-heart talk with Mimì was out of the question. If Mimì did have a woman, he would deny it. He was capable of claiming he went out at night to help the homeless. That he'd felt suddenly overwhelmed by an urge to be charitable. No, first it had to be confirmed with absolute certainty that Mimì had a mistress, and he had to find out when and where these nocturnal trysts took place. But how? The inspector needed someone to lend him a hand. But who could he talk to about this? He certainly couldn't get anyone from the police department mixed up in it, not even Fazio. It had to remain a strictly private matter between Mimì, him, and, at the very most, a third person. A friend. Yes, only a friend could help him out. And he thought of the right person for the job. But he slept badly just the same, waking up three or four times with a big lump of melancholy in his chest.

*

The next morning he called Catarella at the station and told him he'd be coming in a bit later than usual. Then he waited until ten o'clock, an acceptably civilized hour to wake a lady, and made his second phone call of the morning.

'Hello? Who are you?'

It was a low voice. With a Russian accent. Probably an ex-general of the Red Army born in some former Soviet republic beyond Siberia. One of Ingrid's specialities was hiring domestic servants from lands so obscure you had to look them up in an atlas to find out where they were.

'Who are you?' the general repeated imperiously.

Despite his concerns, Montalbano felt like messing around.

'Look, my parents gave me what you might call a provisional name, but who I really am in fact is not so easy to say. I'm not sure if I've made myself clear.'

'You make very clear. You have existential doubt? You lost identity and now cannot find?'

Montalbano felt bewildered. How could he possibly discuss philosophy with an ex-general so early in the morning?

'Look, I'm sorry. This is a fascinating discussion, but I don't have much time at the moment. Is Ingrid there?'

'Yes. But first you tell me provisional name.'

'Montalbano. Salvo Montalbano.'

He had to wait a while. This time, in addition to the times table for seven, he revised the one for eight. And after that, for six as well.

'Forgive me, Salvo, I was in the shower. How nice to hear from you!'

'Who's the general?'

'What general?'

'The one who answered the phone.'

'He's not a general! His name's Igor, he's a former philosophy professor.'

'And what's he doing at your place?'

'He's earning a living, Salvo. Working as my butler. When they had Communism in Russia, he was a virulent anti-Communist. And so first he was forbidden to teach, and then he ended up in prison. And when he got out, he went hungry.'

'But Russia's no longer Communist.'

'Of course, but in the meantime he became a Communist. A revolutionary Communist. And so he was forbidden to teach again. So he decided to emigrate. But tell me about yourself. It's been ages since I last saw you. I really would like to, you know.'

'We can meet tonight, if you want — if you're not already engaged.'

'I can get free. Shall we go out to dinner?'

'Yes. Meet me at eight, at the Marinella Bar.'

FIVE

He hadn't taken a single step before the phone rang.

'Ahh, Chief! Ahh, Chief, Chief!'

Bad sign. Catarella was reciting the commissionerial lamentations.

'What's wrong?'

'Ahh, Chief, Chief! The c'missioner called! An' 'e was angry as a buff'lo! Smoke was comin' out 'is nostrils!'

'Wait a second, Cat. Whoever told you buffalos blow smoke out of their nostrils when they get angry?'

'Ivrybody says so, Chief. I even seen it on TV, in cartoons.'

'OK, OK. What did he want?'

'He says as how you gotta go to his office, the c'mmissioner's office, emergently right now! Jeesus, was 'e ever mad, Chief!'

*

And why should Bonetti-Alderighi be mad at him, he asked himself on his way to Montelusa. Lately there had been dead calm at work: only a few robberies, a few kidnappings, a few shootouts, a few torched cars and shops. The only new development had been the discovery of the body in the bag, too recent to provide the c'mishner with any reason to be angry. More than worried, the inspector was curious.

The first person he encountered in the corridor leading to the commissioner's office was the priestlike, cloying cabinet chief, Dr Lattes, also known as 'honeyed Lattes'. As soon as he saw the inspector, Lattes opened his arms, like the Pope when he greets the throng from his window.

'Dear Inspector!'

And he ran up to Montalbano, grasped his hand, shook it vigorously, and, immediately changing expression, asked him in a conspiratorial tone:

'Any news of the wife?'

Lattes was fixated on the misconception that the inspector was married with children, and there was no way to convince him otherwise. Montalbano froze in terror at the question. What the hell had he said last time they met? Luckily, he remembered he'd confessed that his wife had run off with an immigrant. Moroccan? Tunisian? He couldn't remember the details. He slapped a smile of contentment on his face.

'Ah, good Dr Lattes! I have excellent news! My wife is back under the conjugal roof.'

Dr Lattes went into raptures.

'How wonderful! How very wonderful! Giving thanks to the Blessed Virgin, the home fires are burning again!'

'Yes, and it's getting pretty toasty in there now! We're even saving on the utilities bills!'

Lattes gave him a puzzled look. He hadn't quite understood. Then he said: 'I'll let the commissioner know you're here.'

He disappeared, then reappeared.

'The commissioner will see you now.'

But he was still a bit perplexed.

Bonetti-Alderighi did not look up from the papers he was reading, and did not invite him to sit down. At last he leaned back in his chair and looked at the inspector a long time without saying anything.

'Do you find me very different from the last time we saw each other?' Montalbano asked him, donning a worried expression.

He bit his tongue. Why could he never resist provoking the commissioner whenever he found himself before him?

'Montalbano, how old are you?'

'I was born in 1950. You do the maths.'

'So we can say you're a mature man.'

If I'm mature, then you must be over the hill, Montalbano thought. But he said:

'If you want to say so, go right ahead.'

'Then can you explain to me why you behave like a child?'

What was that supposed to mean? When had he behaved like a child? A quick review of his recent memories brought nothing to mind.

'I don't understand.'

'Then let me explain a little better.'

The commissioner picked up a book, under which was a tiny piece of paper with torn edges. He handed this to the inspector. It was the start of a letter, a phrase of a word and a half, but Montalbano immediately recognized the handwriting. It belonged to Burlando, a former police commissioner, who had written to him often after retiring. So how had this scrap of an old letter ended up in Bonetti-Alderighi's hands? Whatever the case, what did that word and a half have to do with the accusation that he had behaved like a child? Montalbano assumed a defensive stance, just in case.

'What's this piece of paper supposed to mean?' he asked, his expression halfway between shock and surprise.

'Don't you recognize the handwriting?'

'No.'

'Would you read it aloud, please?'

'Certainly. "*Dear Mont*". That's all it says.'

'And in your opinion, what might the whole name be?'

'I dunno, but I could take a few guesses. Dear Montale – who would be the poet. Dear Montanelli – who would be the journalist. Dear Montezuma – who was king of the Aztecs. Dear Montgomery – who was that English general who—'

'How about "Dear Montalbano"?'

'That, too.'

'Listen, Montalbano. Let's stop beating around the bush. This scrap of paper was sent to me by the newsman Pippo Ragonese, who found it inside a rubbish bag.'

Montalbano made a face of utter astonishment.

'So now even Ragonese's taken to rummaging through rubbish bags? It's a kind of addiction, you know. You have no idea how many people – even well-to-do people, you know – go about in the middle of the night, from house to house—'

'I'm not interested in the habits of certain people,' the commissioner cut him short. 'The fact of the matter is that Ragonese recovered this scrap from one of two rubbish bags that were left for him in a certain place by a bogus phone-caller seeking revenge.'

Apparently the piece of paper had been among all the rubbish he'd collected under the veranda, and he hadn't noticed it.

'Mr Commissioner, you'll have to excuse me, but frankly I haven't understood a single word you've said. In what way does this constitute revenge? If you could clarify a little—'

The commissioner sighed.

'A few days ago, you see, when the newsman reported

the story of the dead body found in the rubbish bag, he mentioned that you had neglected to consider another similar bag that contained instead . . .' He interrupted himself, as the explanation was getting complicated. 'Did you see the programme?' he asked, hopefully.

'No, sorry to say.'

'Well, then, let's forget the whys and wherefores. The fact is, Ragonese is convinced that it was you who did this, to offend him.'

'Me? To offend him? How?'

'One of the two bags contained a sheet of paper with the word SHIT written on it.'

'But, Mr Commissioner, if you'll excuse my saying so, there are literally billions of shits in the world! Why is Ragonese such a shit as to think that this one refers specifically to him?'

'Because it would prove—'

'Prove?! What would it prove, Mr Commissioner?'

And, pointing a trembling finger at Bonetti-Alderighi, with an expression of indignation and a quasi-castrato voice, he launched into the climax:

'Ah, so you, Mr Commissioner, actually *believed* such a groundless accusation? Ah, I feel so insulted and humiliated! You're accusing me of an act – no, indeed, a crime – that, if true, would warrant severe punishment! As if I were a common idiot or gambler! That journalist must be possessed to think such a thing!'

End of climax. The inspector inwardly congratulated

himself. He had managed to utter a statement using only titles of novels by Dostoyevsky. Had the commissioner noticed? Of course not! The man was ignorant as a goat.

'Don't get so upset, Montalbano! Come on, in the end—'

'Come on, my eye! In the end, my eye! That man has insulted me! You know what I say, Mr Commissioner? I demand an immediate apology, and in writing, from Mr Ragonese! Actually, no. I want a public apology, broadcast on television! Otherwise I will call a press conference and expose the whole matter! All of it!'

The implied message for the commissioner: And I will tell everyone that you believed the whole story, arsehole.

'Oh, calm down, Montalbano. Just take a deep breath. I'll see what I can do.'

But the inspector, in his fury, had already opened the office door. Closing it behind him, he found his path blocked by Lattes.

'I'm sorry, Inspector, but I didn't quite understand what the connection was between your wife's return home and the utilities bills.'

'I'll explain another time, Doctor.'

*

At Enzo's trattoria he decided he should celebrate the success of the drama he had performed for the commissioner. And that he should continue to distract himself from the worry that Livia's phone call had caused him.

ANDREA CAMILLERI

'Hello, Inspector. For antipasto today we've got frit-
ters of *nunnatu*.'

'I want 'em.'

He committed a massacre of *nunnati* – newborns, that
is. Herod had nothing on him.

'What would you like for a first course, Inspector?
We've got pasta in squid ink, pasta with prawns, with sea
urchin, with mussels, with—'

'With sea urchin.'

'For the second course we've got striped red mullet,
which you can have cooked in salt, fired, roasted, with a
sauce of—'

'Roasted.'

'Will that be all, Inspector?'

'No. Have you got *purpitteddro a strascinasale*?'

'But, Inspector, that's an antipasto.'

'And if I eat it as a post-pasto, what'll happen? Will
you start crying?'

He left the trattoria feeling rather *aggravated*, as the
ancient Romans used to say.

The customary stroll to the lighthouse repaired the
damage, but only in part.

*

The pleasure of his feast immediately vanished when he
entered the station. Upon seeing him, Catarella bent over
as if to search for something on the floor and greeted
him from that position, without looking at him. A rather

ridiculous, infantile move. Why didn't he want to show his face? The inspector pretended not to notice, went into his office, and called him on the phone.

'Catarella, could you come into my office for a moment?'

As soon as Cat entered the room, Montalbano looked at him and realized his eyes were red and moist.

'Do you have a fever?' he asked him.

'No, Chief.'

'What's wrong? Were you crying?'

'A li'l bit, Chief.'

'Why?'

'Iss nuthin', Chief. I's jess cryin'.'

And he blushed from the lie he'd just told.

'Is Inspector Augello here?'

'Yessir, Chief. Fazio's 'ere too.'

'Get me Fazio.'

So now even Catarella was hiding things from him? And suddenly nobody was his friend any more? Why was everyone giving him the run-around? Had he perhaps become the old, tired lion who gets kicked around even by donkeys? This hypothesis, which seemed very likely, made his hands tingle with rage.

'Fazio, come in, shut the door, and sit down.'

'Chief, I've got two things to tell you.'

'No, wait. First I want to know why Catarella was crying when I came in just now.'

'Did you ask him?'

'Yes, but he didn't want to tell me.'

'So why are you asking me?'

So Fazio, too, was kicking him around now? A rage gripped him so furiously that the room started spinning around him like a merry-go-round. Instead of crying out, he roared. A kind of low, deep roar. And, with a leap he wouldn't have thought himself capable of making any more, in a flash he found himself standing upright on top of the desk, from where he flew like a torpedo at Fazio – who, eyes bulging in terror, tried to stand up, got tangled in his chair, which fell, and so failed to get out of the way in time. Thus bearing the full brunt of Montalbano's body, he crashed to the floor with the inspector on top of him. They lay there, arms around each other, for a moment. If someone walked in he might even think they were doing lewd things. Fazio didn't move until Montalbano got up with some effort and, ashamed, went over to the window and looked outside. He was breathing heavily.

Without a word, Fazio set the chair back upright and sat down in it.

A moment later, Montalbano turned around, went up to Fazio, put his hand on his shoulder and said: 'I apologize.'

Fazio then did something he would never have dared do in ordinary circumstances. He laid his hand, palm down, on top of the inspector's hand and said: 'I'm the one who should apologize, Chief. It was I who provoked you.'

Montalbano went and sat back down behind his desk. They looked each other long in the eye. Then Fazio spoke.

'Chief, for a while now, it's been unliveable around here.'

'You mean Augello?'

'Yes, Chief. I see you've caught on. He's completely changed. He used to be cheerful, happy-go-lucky, but now he's always gloomy, he takes offence at the smallest things, he criticizes everything and insults everyone. Vaccarella wanted to go to the union for help, but I managed to persuade him not to. But things can't go on like this much longer. You have to intervene, Chief, and find out what's up with him. Maybe his marriage is turning sour or something . . .'

'Why didn't you say anything to me earlier?'

'Chief, nobody likes to rat on people around here.'

'And what happened with Catarella?'

'He didn't put a call through to Inspector Augello, because he thought he wasn't back in his office yet. Then she called again and Catarella put her through.'

'Why do you say "she"?'

'Because Catarella said it was a woman.'

'Name?'

'Catarella said that both times she called she said only, "Inspector Augello, please."'

'Then what happened?'

'Augello came out of his office looking like he was

75

crazy, grabbed Catarella by the collar, and pushed him up against the wall, screaming, "Why didn't you put the first call through to me?" It's a good thing I was there to pull him back. And it's a good thing there wasn't anyone else, or there would have been trouble. They would surely have reported it to the union.'

'But he's never done anything like that when I'm around.'

'When you're around, Chief, he controls himself.'

So that was how it was. Mimì no longer confided in him, Catarella neither, Fazio had snapped at him ... An uneasy situation that had been dragging on for some time without his even noticing. Once upon a time he'd been attuned to the slightest change of mood in his men and become immediately concerned and wanted to know the reason. Now he didn't even notice any more. He had, of course, seen the change in Mimì, but that was only because it was so obvious that it would have been impossible not to. What was wrong with him? Was he tired? Or had old age made his antennae less sensitive? And, if so, clearly the time had come to pick up his marching orders. But first he had to resolve the problem of Mimì.

'What were the two things you wanted to tell me?' he asked.

Fazio seemed relieved to change the subject.

'Well, Chief, since the start of the year, in Sicily, there've been eighty-two missing persons reported, thirty of whom were female. Which means fifty-two were male. I've done a little sifting. Mind if I look at some notes?'

'As long as you don't start reading me vital statistics, fine.'

'Of these fifty-two, thirty-one are non-Europeans with their papers in order who didn't show up to work from one day to the next and didn't go back to their place of residence either. Of the remaining twenty-one, ten are children. Which leaves eleven. Of these eleven, eight are between seventy and almost ninety years old. All of them are no longer all really there, the kind that might leave the house and not be able to find the way back.'

'Which leaves us with how many?'

'Three, Chief. Of these three – all of whom are around forty – one is five foot two, the second is six foot four, and the third has a pacemaker.'

'And so?'

'And so none of these reports concerns our corpse.'

'And now, what should I do to you?'

Fazio looked flummoxed.

'Why should you want to do something to me, Chief?'

'Because you wasted so many words. Didn't you know that wasting words is a crime against humanity? You could have simply said to me: "Look, none of the people who have been reported missing corresponds to our body in the bag." That would have synthesized the whole thing, and we both would have saved something: you, your breath, and me, my time. Don't you agree?'

Fazio shook his head negatively.

'With all due respect, sir, no.'

'And why not?'

'My dear Inspector, no "synthesis", as you call it, could ever give a sense of all the work that went into arriving at that synthesis.'

'All right, you win. And what was the other thing?'

'Do you remember that when I told you what I'd found out about Dolores Alfano, I said I couldn't remember something somebody had told me?'

'Yes. Do you remember now?'

'Among the people I talked to, there was also an old retired shopkeeper who told me that Giovanni Alfano, Dolores's husband, was Filippo Alfano's son.'

'So?'

'When he told me, I didn't attach any importance to it. It's something that goes back to before you started working here. This Filippo Alfano was a big cheese in the Sinagra family. He was also a distant relative.'

'Whoa!'

The Sinagras were one of the two historic Mafia families of Vigàta. The other was the Cuffaro family.

'At a certain point this Filippo Alfano disappeared. He resurfaced in Colombia with his wife and son, Giovanni, who at the time wasn't yet fifteen years old. Of course, Filippo Alfano didn't leave the country legally. He didn't have a passport, and he had three serious convictions. Around town they said the Sinagras had sent him abroad to look after their interests in Bogotá. But after he'd been there a while, Filippo Alfano was shot and killed; nobody ever found out by whom. And there you have it.'

'What do you mean, "There you have it"?'

'I mean that's the end of the story, Chief. Giovanni Alfano, Dolores's husband, works as a ship's officer and has a clean record, absolutely spotless. Why, do the sons of Mafiosi always have to become Mafiosi like their fathers?'

'No. So, if Giovanni Alfano is clean, then the attempt to run over his wife can't have been an indirect vendetta or a warning. It must have been a nasty prank or drunken antic. Do you agree?'

'I agree.'

*

The inspector was thinking of going home to change for his meeting with Ingrid when he heard Galluzzo's voice asking permission to enter.

'Come in, come in.'

Galluzzo entered and shut the door behind him. He had an envelope in his hand.

'What is it?' Montalbano asked.

'Inspector Augello told me to give you this.'

He put the envelope on the desk. It wasn't closed. On the outside, in block letters printed by a computer, it said: 'FOR CHIEF INSPECTOR SALVO MON-TALBANO.' And below: 'Personal and Confidential.' And in the upper left corner: 'From Domenico Augello.'

Montalbano didn't take out the letter. He looked at Galluzzo and asked:

'Is Inspector Augello still in his office?'

'No, Chief, he left about half an hour ago.'

'Why did you take half an hour to bring me this letter?'

Galluzzo was visibly embarrassed.

'Well, it wasn't . . .' he began to say.

'Did he tell you to wait half an hour before bringing it to me?'

'No, Chief, it took me that long to understand what he had written by hand on the sheet of paper he told me to type up and bring to you. A lot of stuff was crossed out and some of the words were hard to work out. When I finished, I went back to his office to ask him to sign it, but he'd already left. So I decided to bring it to you anyway, without his signature.'

He reached into his jacket pocket, pulled out a sheet of paper, and laid it down beside the envelope.

'This is the original.'

'OK. You can go.'

SIX

The letter said:

Dear Salvo,
*   As I've already brought directly to your attention, the*
situation that has developed between us needs to be fully clarified,
without any holding back or beating around the bush. I believe
that after so many years of working together — where I, however,
have always played a subordinate role — the time has come for
me to have my own autonomous space. I am convinced that the
investigation into the as-yet-unidentified, dismembered forty-
year-old man could be a sort of decisive test for the two of us.
In other words: I want you to assign the case exclusively to
me, and for you to step completely aside. *Naturally, it will*
be my responsibility to keep you up to date on everything, but
you must not interfere in any way. I am even willing, once the
case is closed, to give you publicly all the credit.
*   This isn't a diktat. Please try to understand me: if anything,*
what I am asking of you is some proof of your esteem for me.

And some help, as well. Naturally, it will also be a test, however difficult, of my abilities.

Should you not be in agreement, I shall have no choice but to ask the commissioner to transfer me elsewhere.

Whatever you decide, my great affection and esteem for you will always remain unchanged.

With love,

There was no signature, as Galluzzo had already said. But it was too late now to think all this over.

He slipped the letter into his jacket pocket and wiped his eyes (Ah, old age! How easily the emotions get stirred up!). He stood up and went out.

*

At the Marinella Bar he found Ingrid sitting at a table, having already drunk her first glass of whisky. The five or six male customers couldn't take their eyes off her. How was it that the more the years went by, the more beautiful she became? Beautiful, elegant, intelligent, discreet. A true friend. Of all the times he had asked her for help in a case, she had never asked a single question, never asked why or what for, but had only done what she'd been asked to do.

They embraced, genuinely happy to see each other.

'Shall we leave straight away or order another whisky?' Ingrid asked.

'There's no hurry,' said Montalbano, sitting down.

Ingrid took one of the inspector's hands in hers and squeezed it. That was another good thing about her: she displayed her feelings openly, without worrying about what others might think.

'How did you get here? I didn't see your car in the car park.'

'The red one, you mean? I got rid of it. Now I have a perfectly normal green Nissan Micra. How's Livia?'

'I talked to her yesterday. She's well. How's your husband?'

'I think he's well, too. I haven't seen him for a week. We live apart, even at home. Fortunately the house is very big. Anyway, ever since he became a deputy in Parliament, he spends more time in Rome than here.'

Ingrid's husband was a known ne'er-do-well, so it was only logical that he should turn to politics. The inspector recalled a popular saying from his childhood, which an uncle of his used to repeat: *If you have no art or trade, in politics you'll make the grade.*

'Shall we talk now or after dinner?' asked Ingrid.

'Talk about what?'

'Salvo, stop acting. You only call on me when you need me to do something for you. Isn't that so?'

'You're right. And I'm sorry.'

'Don't be sorry. It's the way you are. And in fact that's one of the reasons I like you. So, do you want to talk about it now or later?'

'Do you know that Mimì is married now?'

Ingrid laughed.

'Of course. With Beba. And I also know they have a son, whom they named Salvo, after you.'

'Who told you?'

'Mimì. He used to call me every now and then. We've even met a few times. But I haven't heard from him for a couple of months. So?'

'I have reason to believe that Mimì has a mistress,' said the inspector.

Ingrid didn't bat an eyelash. Montalbano marvelled.

'What? Aren't you going to say anything?'

Suddenly it dawned on him.

'You knew?' he asked.

'Yes.'

'Did he tell you himself?'

'No. In fact, nobody told me, not before you did just now. But, you see, Salvo, wasn't this to be expected, knowing what Mimì is like? What's wrong, Salvo? Are you scandalized?'

And she started laughing harder than before. Maybe the two glasses of whisky were already beginning to make themselves felt?

Ingrid read his mind. 'No, I'm not tipsy, Salvo. It's just that you have such a serious expression on your face that I can't help but laugh. Why do you take it so hard? It's a very normal thing, you know. I don't need to tell you that. Just leave him in peace and the whole thing will blow over by itself.'

'I can't.'

And he told her about Livia's phone call and Mimì's excuse for spending the night away from home.

'Don't you see? If I don't intervene, Beba will eventually come directly to me. And at that point I won't be able to cover for him any longer. And there's another thing about Mimì that has me very worried.'

'Before you tell me, let's have another round.'

'No, just order for yourself.'

He told her how Mimì had changed, how he blew up at others for no reason, always seeking conflict to let off steam.

'There are two possibilities,' said Ingrid. 'Either he's upset by the situation because he loves Beba and feels guilty, or else he's fallen seriously in love with this other woman. All of this assuming, of course, that Mimì has a lover, as you say. But isn't it possible he's going out at night for some other reason?'

'I don't think so.'

'So what do you want from me?'

'I want you to find out if Mimì really does have a mistress. And, if possible, who this woman is. I'll give you his licence number, so you can follow him.'

'But I can hardly stake out Mimì's house every night, waiting for him to—'

'You won't have to. I've done a little calculation, based on what Livia told me, and I'm certain he'll be going out tomorrow night. Do you know where he lives?'

'Yes. And I've got nothing on for tomorrow night. So, what do I do after he comes out?'

'You call me at home. No matter the hour.'

He waited for Ingrid to finish her whisky, and then they left the bar.

'My car or yours?' asked Ingrid.

'Mine. You've been drinking.'

'But I can hold it perfectly well!'

'Yes, but if we get stopped, it'll be hard to explain and convince them of that. We'll come and pick up your car afterwards.'

Ingrid looked at him and smiled, then got into his car.

*

When they got to the restaurant, Peppucciu 'u piscaturi, which was on the road to Fiacca, it was almost ten o'clock. The inspector had reserved a table because the place was always packed, and knowing Ingrid's tastes, and that she was a good eater, he had even ordered their dishes in advance, certain that she would approve.

The menu: antipasto di mare (fresh anchovies cooked in lemon juice and dressed in olive oil, salt, pepper and parsley; 'savoury' anchovies seasoned with fennel seeds; octopus salad; and fried whitebait); first course: spaghetti with coral sauce; second course: spiny lobster marinara (cooked over live coals and dressed in olive oil, salt, and a dash of pepper).

They dispatched three bottles of treacherous white wine, which went down like cool water but, once in the system, shifted into high gear and was off like a shot. When they had finished they each drank a whisky to give the digestive process a little boost.

'And now, if we get pulled over, how are you going to explain that you can hold your wine?'

He laughed.

The whole way back, Montalbano drove with his eyes popping out and his nerves on edge. Afraid they might encounter a local patrol, he didn't go over thirty-five miles an hour, and he didn't once open his mouth, for fear of distraction.

Pulling into the car park of the Marinella Bar, he realized Ingrid had fallen asleep. He shook her gently.

'Hmm?' Ingrid said without opening her eyes.

'We're here. You feel up to driving?'

Ingrid opened a single eye and looked around her, dazed.

'What did you say?'

'I asked if you felt up to driving.'

'No.'

'All right, then, I'll take you home to Montelusa.'

'No. Take me to your place and I'll have a shower, and then you can bring me back here for my car.'

As Montalbano was opening the front door, Ingrid was swaying so badly she had to lean against the wall for support.

'I'm going to lie down for five minutes,' she said, heading for the bedroom.

The inspector didn't follow her. He opened the French windows, went out onto the veranda, and sat down on the bench.

There wasn't a breath of wind; the surf was so soft, the sea barely moving. At that moment the telephone rang. Montalbano dashed in to close the bedroom door, then picked up the receiver. It was Livia.

'Tell me something,' she said. 'What were you doing?'

She sounded like Torquemada. Women! Never before had Livia initiated a phone conversation with a question like that. Tonight, however, when another woman was sleeping in her man's bed, she came out with this inquisitorial tone. What was it? A sixth, animal sense? Or did she have telescopic X-ray vision? He felt spooked, which muddled his brain, and instead of telling her the truth – that he was sitting and watching the sea – for God knows what reason he replied with a pointless, idiotic lie.

'I was watching a film on television.'

'What channel?'

She must have realized at once that he was speaking falsely. They'd been together for years, and by now Livia could tell, from the slightest inflection of his voice, whether he was telling the truth or not. So how was he going to wiggle out of this now? The only hope was to continue down the same path.

'Three. But what—'

'I'm watching it too. What's it called?'

'I don't know, it had already started when I turned it on. But what's with all these questions? What's got into you?'

'Why are you speaking softly?'

She was right, dammit! He was keeping his voice down instinctively, so as not to wake Ingrid. He cleared his throat.

'Am I? I hadn't noticed.'

'Who's there with you?'

'Nobody! Who could possibly be here with me?'

'Never mind. Beba called me. Mimì told her he would have to do another stake-out tomorrow night.'

Good. That meant he had calculated correctly.

'Did you tell Beba to be patient a little while longer?'

'Yes. But you're not being straight with me.'

'What am I not being straight—'

'You're not alone.'

Jesus, what a nose! What, did she have antennae or something? Did she talk to the dead?

'Come on, knock it off!'

'Swear it!'

'If you really care that much, I swear it.'

'Bah. Good night.'

Well, that was that. Livia had got what she deserved. She had pushed things so far that he, in all innocence, had been forced to lie to her, and to swear to the lie. In all innocence? Not so fast! In reality he wasn't all that innocent. Livia had been right on target. It was true there was another person there with him, and a woman at that, but how could he ever have explained to her that this woman wasn't . . . He imagined how their conversation would have gone.

'But she's sleeping in our *bed!'*

Dammit and dammit again! She was right. That bed was not just his; it was both of theirs.

'Yes, but, you see, she's going to leave afterwards.'

'Afterwards? After what?'

Forget it.

He went back out on the veranda and sat down. Reaching into his pocket, he dug out Mimì's letter, which he had brought with him to show Ingrid, later changing his mind. He didn't re-read it, but only stared at the envelope, thinking.

Why had Mimì had Galluzzo copy a letter so personal and confidential? This was one of the first questions he had asked himself when Galluzzo brought it to him. Mimì could very well have typed it up himself, stuck it in an envelope and had someone pass it on to him, if he really didn't want to do it in person.

Didn't Mimì realize that in so doing he was involving a third party in the delicate situation between the two of them? And then, why choose Galluzzo of all people, who had a loose tongue and a journalist for a brother-in-law?

Wait a minute. Maybe there was an explanation. What if, in fact, Mimì had done it on purpose? Steady, Montalbà, you're almost there.

Mimì had acted in this fashion because he wanted others to know about the matter – because he wanted it to have a certain amount of publicity.

And why would he do that? Simple: because he wanted to put his – Montalbano's – back to the wall. In so doing, the matter could no longer be resolved in secret, behind closed doors, far from the eyes of others. No, in this way Mimì would force him to give an official reply, whatever it was. Smart move, no doubt about it.

He picked up the envelope, pulled out the letter, and re-read it. There were at least two things that caught his attention.

The first was the tone.

When Mimì had asked him in person what his intentions were as to who should conduct the investigation, ruling out any possibility of collaboration, he was aggressive, rude, obnoxious, scornful.

In the letter, on the other hand, his tone had changed. Here, in fact, he presented the reasons for his request, explaining that he needed space and total autonomy. He let it be known that there wasn't enough breathing room for him in the police department. And this was understandable. Mimì had been working for many years under him, and very rarely had he given him free rein. He had to be honest and recognize this.

In the letter he also said that by entrusting the case to him, the inspector could put all his abilities to the test.

In conclusion, Mimì was asking for help.

Exactly that. He even used the word: *help*. A word that a man like Mimì didn't use lightly.

Think harder, Montalbà, try to reflect with an open mind, without anger, without falling prey to resentment.

Wasn't it possible that Mimì's aggressive, belligerent attitude was his own very personal way of calling to other people's attention a situation he couldn't get out of alone?

All right, let's admit this. Then what did the investigation have to do with it? Why was Mimì so fixated on it? Why had it become, from one day to the next, so important to his very existence?

One possible answer might be that once he was involved in a difficult, complex investigation, Mimì would inevitably find he had less time to spend on his mistress. And so he could ease up on his relations with the woman, take the first steps towards a definitive break.

Ingrid was probably on target when she said that Mimì might be falling seriously in love and wanted to prevent it, since Beba and the baby were caught in the middle.

He read the letter a third time.

When he got to the last sentence — *Whatever you should decide, my great affection and esteem for you will always remain unchanged* — he immediately felt his eyes water and his chest tighten up. Mimì had written 'affection' first, and 'esteem' after.

The inspector buried his face in his hands, finally giving full vent to his sadness – and to his anger at not having immediately grasped, as he would have done a few years earlier, the gravity of his friend's predicament, who was so much a friend that he named his first son after him.

At that moment he felt Ingrid's presence on the veranda.

He hadn't heard her approach, convinced she was still asleep. He didn't look at her, too embarrassed at having been caught by surprise at a moment of weakness he was unable to bring to an end.

Then Ingrid turned off the light.

And it was as though at the same time she had turned on the sea, which now emitted a pale, almost phosphorescent glow, and the distant, scattered lights of the stars.

From an invisible boat, a man cried out:

'Giuvà! Giuvà!'

But no one replied.

Absurdly, the reply that never came was like the last painful rent in Montalbano's chest. He started weeping without restraint.

Ingrid sat down on the bench beside him, held him tight, and made it so that Montalbano could rest his head on her shoulder.

Then, with her left hand she raised his chin and gave him a long kiss on the lips.

✻

It was six o'clock in the morning when he drove Ingrid back to the Marinella Bar to pick up her car.

He didn't feel like sleeping. On the contrary, he felt an overwhelming need to clean himself, to have a shower so long it would use up all the water in the tanks. When he got home, he undressed, put on his trunks, and went down to the beach.

It was cold. It was a little while before sunrise, and a light wind made of billions of little steel blades was blowing.

Like almost every morning, Cosimo Lauricella was easing back into the water the boat he had pulled ashore the previous evening. He was an elderly fisherman who every so often brought the inspector fresh-caught fish and never accepted any payment.

'Isspector, I don' think iss such a good idea this morning.'

'Just a little dip, Cosimo.'

He stepped into the water, overcame an immediate attack of paralysis, dived under, and had taken a few strokes when all at once the night's darkness returned.

How is that possible? he had just enough time to think before feeling the sea water rush into his mouth.

He woke up in Cosimo's boat with the fisherman pounding him with his fist.

'Shit, Isspector, you sure gave me a scare! I tol' you it wasn't such a good idea today! Good thing I was here, or you woulda drownded!'

Once ashore, Cosimo wanted to accompany him all the way home and wouldn't take no for an answer.

'No more o' these pranks, Isspector, I mean it. Iss one thing when you're a kid, but iss another thing later on.'

'Thanks, Cosimo,' he said. But he was thinking: *Thanks not so much for having saved my life as for not having called me an old man.*

But, as the saying goes, if it looks like a duck, swims like a duck, and quacks like a duck, then it probably is a duck.

Mature, elderly, of a certain age, no longer young, getting on in years: all ways to soften but not change an essential fact – that he was getting unavoidably, irreme- diably old.

He went into the kitchen, put a six-cup espresso pot on the stove, then drank the scalding-hot coffee from a large milk-bowl.

Afterwards he got into the shower and used up all the water, imagining Adelina's curses when she realized she couldn't clean the house or scrub the floors, probably not even cook.

In the end he felt a little cleaner.

*

'Ah, Chief, Chief! Dacter Arcà's been lookin' f'yiz an' he sez a tell yiz a call 'im at Frensix.'

'All right. I'll tell you when I want you to ring him for me.'

First he needed to do something more urgent.

He went into his office, locked the door behind him, sat down at his desk, dug Mimì's letter out of his pocket, and read it one more time.

The previous evening, when he had started mulling over Mimì's words, he was struck by two things. The first was the tone, and the second . . .

The second had slipped his mind because Ingrid had woken up. And even now, try as he might, he could not recall it.

And so he took a ballpoint pen and a clean sheet of paper without letterhead, thought things over a bit, and started writing.

SEVEN

Dear Mimi,

I have read your letter very carefully.

It did not surprise me, given your attitude over the last few weeks.

I even understand, in part, your reasons for writing it.

And thus I am (almost) convinced I should meet you halfway.

But don't you think that asking me for total freedom and autonomy in investigating the critaru case, of all things, might be a mistake on your part?

You know I consider you a skilful, intelligent detective. But this seems to me the sort of case that might baffle a policeman even better than the two of us put together.

If I hesitate to turn it over to you, it is precisely because I am your friend.

Because, were you to fail, it would create endless complications, and not only in our personal relations.

Think it over.

At any rate, if your mind remains unchanged, allow me a few days to decide.

With unwavering affection,
    Salvo

He re-read the letter. It seemed perfect.

It would help keep Mimì in line for a few days, while the inspector awaited the results of Ingrid's surveillance. And it gave him no reason to get angry and commit any more gaffes.

He got up, opened the door, and called Galluzzo.

'Listen, do me a favour and type up this letter. Then put it in an envelope and write "For Inspector Domenico Augello / Personal and Confidential" on it. Then deliver it to him. Is he in his office?'

Galluzzo only gawked at him, bewildered. No doubt he was wondering why Montalbano and Augello had suddenly decided to use him as their personal secretary.

'He hasn't come in yet.'

'Give it to him as soon as he arrives.'

But Galluzzo made no move to leave the room. He clearly felt torn.

'Is anything wrong?'

'Well, yes, Chief. Could you tell me why you, too, are having me type up a letter?'

'So that you know exactly how things stand. You've read the one Mimì wrote to me, and now you can read my reply,' he said sharply – so sharply that Galluzzo reacted.

'Excuse me for saying so, Chief, but I don't understand. First of all, you can't type up a letter without reading it. And, second, after I know how things stand between the two of you, what am I supposed to do about it?'

'I don't know. You decide.'

'Chief, you've got me all wrong,' said Galluzzo, offended. 'I'm not the type who goes around telling everybody and his dog what goes on here.'

Montalbano felt Galluzzo was being sincere and immediately regretted what he'd said. But the damage had been done. Directly or indirectly, Mimì Augello was sowing discord and resentment in his police department. The problem had to be resolved as quickly as possible. Meanwhile, he could only hope that Ingrid would discover something.

'Catarella! Ring Forensics for me and get Dr Arquà on the line!'

'Hello,' said Arquà after a spell.

'Montalbano here. You asked for me?'

'Yes.'

'What do you want?'

'I want to prove to you that I am a gentleman and you are a boor.'

'An impossible task.'

'Professor Lomascolo called me from Palermo early with the results of his examination of the dental bridge. Interested?'

'Yes.'

'It took him only an hour, he said, to be absolutely certain that this kind of bridge was commonly used in South America until a few years ago. Happy?'

The inspector said nothing. What the hell was the little shit getting at?

'I made a point of letting you know at once,' Arquà continued, shooting the venom from his tail. 'I hope you're able, with your usual acumen, to find the right dentist among the million or more practising in that part of the world. Bye.'

Fucker. Actually, no: motherfucking son of a bitch. Actually, no: motherfucking son of a stinking whore.

If that damned bridge might actually be of any use to the case, never in a million years would he have called him. He only wanted the satisfaction of telling him that the bridge would never help him to cross the great sea of shit this case was.

Maybe it wasn't such a good idea to turn it over to Mimì.

*

It was time to eat, but he didn't have even a hint of an appetite.

His thoughts felt a bit muddled, as if a few drops

of glue had oozed into his brain. He felt his forehead. It was hot. Apparently the result of the morning's bravado.

He decided to go straight home to Marinella and told Catarella he wouldn't be back at the office in the afternoon.

When he got home, he started looking for the thermometer. It wasn't in the medicine chest, where he usually kept it. It wasn't in the drawer of his bedside table either. After searching for twenty minutes he finally found it between the pages of a book. Ninety-nine point five. He took an aspirin from the medicine cabinet, went into the kitchen and turned on the tap, but not a single drop of water came out. He cursed the saints. But why curse the saints when it was his own fault? There was a bottle of mineral water in the refrigerator, and he poured himself a glass. But then he remembered that aspirin should not be taken on an empty stomach. He needed to eat something. He reopened the refrigerator. Lacking water, Adelina had used her brains. *Caponatina*, caciocavallo cheese from Ragusa, and sardines in onion sauce.

Without knowing how or why, he suddenly felt ravenous. He took everything out onto the veranda, along with a bottle of cold white wine. He spent an hour savouring it all. And so, afterwards, he could take the aspirin without worry.

*

When he woke up it was almost five in the afternoon. He took his temperature. Ninety-eight. The aspirin had brought it down. But perhaps it was best to stay in bed. Reading a book, for example.

He got up, went to the bookcase in the living room and started scanning the titles. His eye fell upon a book by Andrea Camilleri from a few years back, which he hadn't yet read. He brought it back to bed with him and started reading it.

Taking off from a passage in a novel by Leonardo Sciascia, the book was about a man named Patò, a serious, upstanding bank manager who amused himself by playing the role of Judas in the annual production of the Mortorio, a popular version of the Passion of Christ.

As is well known, Judas repented after betraying Jesus Christ, throwing the thirty pieces of silver he had received for his treachery into the temple, and ran off to hang himself. And the Mortorio play followed the Gospel story every step of the way. There was, however, one variant in the stage production: as Patò–Judas tightened the noose around his neck, a trapdoor opened under his feet, symbolizing the mouth of Hell, and the betrayer plummeted into this hole, ending up in the understage.

In Camilleri's novel, everything went as it had always done, as if according to script, except for the fact that once the performance was over, Patò never reappeared. Everyone set about looking for him, to no avail. He had vanished for ever after being swallowed up by the trap-door.

The book continued with conjectures, some quite far-fetched, by ordinary people and experts, and an investigation was conducted by a police detective and a marshal of the carabinieri in hopes of resolving the mystery of the disappearance.

After three hours of reading, the inspector's vision started to blur.

Wasn't it perhaps time to have his eyes examined? No, he answered himself, it was not time. He well knew his eyesight wasn't what it used to be, but even were he to turn blind, he would never give in and wear glasses.

He put the book on the bedside table, got out of bed, went into the living room and sat down in the armchair in front of the television. Turning it on, he was greeted by none other than the chicken-arse face of Pippo Ragonese.

'... owning up to our mistakes, on those fortunately rare occasions when we do make mistakes, is the indisputable mark of fairness and good faith on our part. Indeed fairness and good faith are the shining beacons that have always lighted the way during our thirty years of delivering the news. Well, we did recently make one such mistake. We accused Chief Inspector Salvo Montalbano of the Vigàta Police of not pursuing a possible lead in the case of the unknown and dismembered murder victim found in an arid stretch of land called *'u critaru*. This lead turned out to have no connection to that horrific crime. We therefore extend our public apologies to Inspector Montalbano. This does not mean, however, that our reservations as to him and the methods he often applies are thereby diminished. And now I would like to talk about the Town Council of Montereale, which recently . . .'

Montalbano turned it off. So the commissioner had kept his word.

He stood up, feeling restless. He started fidgeting about the house.

There was something in Camilleri's novel that kept buzzing in his brain.

What was it? Was it possible his memory, too, was beginning to fail?

Was this already the start of arteriosclerosis?

He tried hard to remember.

It was definitely something to do with the death of Judas but wasn't actually written in the book.

It was a sort of parallel thought that appeared and vanished like a flash. But if it was a parallel thought, there was no point in re-reading the novel from the start. It was unlikely the flash would repeat itself.

Still, there might be a way.

Somewhere in his library he must have the four Gospels in a single volume. Where were they hidden? Why was everything always disappearing in this house? First the thermometer, now the Gospels . . . At last he found them after half an hour of a panoply of curses unsuitable to the book he wanted to read.

He sat back down in the armchair and looked up, in the first Gospel, that of Matthew, the passage that recounted the suicide of Judas.

> When Judas, his betrayer, saw that he was condemned he repented and brought back the thirty pieces of silver to the chief priests and the elders, saying,
>> 'I have sinned in betraying innocent blood.'
>
> They said, 'What is that to us? See to it yourself.'
>
> And throwing down the pieces of silver in the temple, he departed; and he went and hanged himself.
>
> But the chief priests, taking the pieces of silver, said, 'It is not lawful to put them into the treasury, since they are blood money.'
>
> So they took counsel, and bought with them the potter's field, to bury strangers in . . .

The other Gospels didn't talk about the death of Judas.

Though he didn't quite know why, he was excited. A sort of tremor ran through his whole body. He was like a dog pointing towards its prey. He sensed that there was something of great importance in those lines of Matthew.

With saintly patience he read the verses again, slowly, almost syllable by syllable.

When he reached the words *the potter's field*, he felt an actual shock.

The potter's field.

All at once, he found himself again on a footpath, his clothes drenched with rain, looking out over a valley made up of slabs of clay. And he heard the peasant's words again:

'. . . this place has always been called '*u critaru* . . . I sell the clay to people who make vases, jugs, pots, that kind of thing . . .'

The potter's field. Sicilian translation: '*u critaru*.

That was the parallel thought he'd had.

But did it mean anything? Might it not be a simple coincidence? Wasn't he perhaps getting carried away by his imagination? Fine, but what was wrong with having a little imagination? And how many times had things he'd imagined proved to be real?

Let's allow, then, that this imagining meant something. What could it mean that the body of the murder victim was found in a potter's field? The Gospel said that the priests had bought the field to bury strangers in . . .

Wait a second, Montalbà.

Wasn't it possible the victim was a 'stranger' – in other words, a foreigner? Pasquano had found a bridge in his stomach, and this kind of bridge, according to Professor Lomascolo, was used by dentists in South America. So the stranger was probably from one of those countries – a Venezuelan or Argentinian . . . Or maybe Colombian. A Colombian with Mafia connections to boot . . .

Aren't you maybe sailing too far out to sea, Montalbà?

As he asked himself this question, a cold shudder ran through his body, followed at once by a great wave of heat. He felt his forehead. The fever was rising again. But he didn't worry, because he was certain that this change was due not to influenza but to the ideas percolating in his brain.

Better not push it, however. Better pause a while and calm down. He realized his brain was overheating and ready to melt. He needed to seek distraction. How? The only solution was to watch television. So he turned it back on, but this time tuned in to the Free Channel.

They were broadcasting a soft-core porn film, the kind where the actors and actresses only pretend to fuck, usually in rather uncomfortable places like inside a wheelbarrow or while holding on to a gutter, and they're worse than the hard-core films, in which they actually fuck. He sat and watched it for ten minutes or so and, as always happened, with soft-core as well as hard-core, it put him to sleep. And he slept just like that, head bent backwards, mouth open.

*

He didn't know how long he had slept, but when he woke up, in the place of the porn film were four people around a small table talking about unsolved crimes. But even crimes that appear to have been solved — said a man with moustache and goatee à la d'Artagnan — all remain, in fact, unsolved. And he gave a sly smile and said nothing else. Since none of the other participants had understood a fucking thing of what they had just heard, another guy who was a professional criminologist (Why do criminologists always have Moses-like beards?) began to recount a crime committed in northern Italy, where a woman was murdered with mouse poison and then dismembered.

The same word Pasquano had used. Dismembered.

What had the doctor said about this?

That the body had been cut into a certain number of pieces. Yes, but how many?

He shot to his feet, stunned and sweaty, his fever spiking a few degrees more. He ran to the telephone and dialled.

It rang and rang a long time with no answer. All right, times tables for — come off it! Times tables?! If they didn't pick up the phone he was going to do a Columbine! He was gonna get in the car and shoot them all, one by one! Finally a man's voice answered, sounding so drunk he could smell his breath over the telephone line.

'H'lo? 'Ooziss?'

'Montalbano here. I'd like to speak with Dr Pasquano.'

'M ... morgue's c ... closed a' nnight.'

So he must be at home. A sleepy-sounding woman answered the phone. What the hell time was it?

'Montalbano here. Is the doctor at home?'

'No, Inspector. He's gone to the club.'

'I'm sorry, signora, but have you got the telephone number?'

Pasquano's wife gave it to him, and he dialled it.

'Hello? Montalbano here.'

'What the hell do I care?' said somebody, hanging up.

He must have dialled wrong. All his fingers were trembling and hard to control.

'Montalbano here. Is Dr Pasquano there?'

'I'll see if he can come to the phone.'

Times table for seven. Complete.

'I'm sorry, but he's playing and doesn't want to be disturbed.'

'Listen, tell him either he comes to the phone, or I'm going to show up at his place at five o'clock in the morning with the police department band. The programme will be: first, the triumphal march from *Aida*; second—'

'Wait. I'll go and tell him right away.'

Times table for eight.

'Can't a gentleman sit in peace for a few minutes without you always coming along and breaking his balls? Eh? What fucking way of going about things is this? Are you even aware of it? Eh? Why do you need to come scratching round my door all the time? Eh? What the hell do you want?'

'Did you get it out of your system, Doctor?'

'Not entirely. The pain in the arse is great.'

'May I speak?'

'Yes, but then you must vanish from the face of the earth, because if I run into you, I'm going to perform a post-mortem without anaesthesia.'

'Can you tell me exactly how many pieces the body was cut into?'

'I've forgotten.'

'Please, Doctor.'

'Wait while I do a tally. So, the fingers of both hands and the toes of both feet make twenty ... then the legs ... the ears ... in total, twenty-nine, no, wait. Thirty pieces.'

'Are you sure? Thirty?'

'Absolutely sure.'

That was why they had left one arm attached. Had they cut it off, that would have made thirty-one pieces. Whereas it had to be exactly thirty.

Like Judas's thirty pieces of silver.

*

He could no longer stand the heat he felt inside the house. He got dressed, put on a heavy jacket, and went out on the veranda to think.

That they had a Mafia murder on their hands he had been convinced of from the moment Pasquano told him the stranger had been killed with one shot to the base of the skull. A typical procedure that connected, with an invisible thread, the worst kind of criminal cruelty with certain methods sanctioned by time-honoured military custom.

But here something else was emerging.

Whoever killed the stranger was purposely providing the inspector with precise information as to the whys and wherefores of the killing itself.

Meanwhile, this murder had been committed, or ordered – which amounted to the same thing – by someone who still operated in observance of the rules of the 'old' Mafia.

Why?

The answer was simple: because the new Mafia fired their guns pell-mell and in every direction, at old people and children, wherever and whenever, and never deigned to give a reason or explanation for what they did.

With the old Mafia, it was different. They explained, informed, and clarified. Not, of course, aloud or in print, no. But through signs.

The old Mafia were experts in semiology, the science of signs used to communicate.

Murdered with a thorny branch of prickly pear placed on the body?

We did it because he pricked us one too many time with his thorns and troubles.

Murdered with a stone in his mouth?

We did it because he talked too much.

Murdered with both hands cut off?

We did it because we caught him with his hands in the biscuit tin.

Murdered with his balls shoved into his mouth?

We did it because he was fucking someone he shouldn't have been.

Murdered with his shoes on his chest?

We did it because he wanted to run away.

Murdered with both eyes gouged out?

We did it because he refused to see the obvious.

Murdered with all his teeth pulled out?

We did it because he ate too much.

And so on merrily in this fashion.

For this reason, the meaning of the message was immediately clear to Montalbano: we killed him as he deserved, because he betrayed us for thirty pieces of silver, like Judas.

Thus the logical conclusion was that the murdered stranger was a Mafioso, 'executed' because he was a traitor. Which amounted to, finally, a first step forward.

Wait a second, Montalbà. Maybe you've been touched by divine Grace.

Yes indeed. Because if the argument made sense, and it made beautiful sense, it might be possible to get free of this case, to sidestep it with elegance.

In fact, if the victim was a Mafioso, the matter might not be his concern any more, but the Anti-Mafia Commission's.

He cheered up. Yes, this was the right path to take.

And, most importantly, it got rid of the troublesome question of Mimì.

First thing tomorrow morning, he would go to Montelusa to talk to Musante, a colleague in charge of local Mafia matters.

EIGHT

In the meantime, however, he had to kill some time while waiting for Ingrid's phone call.

He played the only three versions of solitaire he knew, without cheating as he often did. He played over and over, without winning a single hand.

He went to his bookcase to fetch a book Livia had bought, *Solitaire for the Solitary*. The first version belonged to the category the author defined as the easiest. The inspector couldn't even understand how the cards were supposed to be set up. Then he played a game of chess against himself, changing places with each move, so that he would seem like a real opponent. Fortunately, it was a long match. But the opponent won with a brilliant move. And Montalbano felt upset with himself for having lost.

'Care for a rematch?' his adversary asked.

'No, thanks,' Montalbano replied to himself.

His opponent would probably have won the rematch, too.

Careful inspection, in front of the bathroom mirror, of a tiny little pimple beside his nose. Bitter acknowledgement of a certain amount of hair loss. Failed attempt at counting same (approximately, that is).

Second game of chess, also lost, resulting in hurling of various objects against the walls.

*

The phone call never came. Instead, around six o'clock in the morning — by which time, at the end of his tether, he had collapsed on his bed — he heard the sound of a car pulling up in the parking space in front of the house. He raced to open the door. It was Ingrid, half-frozen to death.

'Give me some steaming hot tea. I'm freezing.'

'But weren't you used to much colder—'

'I guess I'm not any more.'

'Tell me what happened.'

'I parked on a side street from where I could keep an eye on Mimì's front door. He came out at ten, got into his car, which was parked right outside, and drove off. He was very agitated.'

'How could you tell?'

'From the way he drove.'

'Here's your tea. Shall we go into the living room?'

'No. Let's stay in the kitchen. Would you believe that for a moment I thought he was coming to see you?'

'Why?'

'Because he was headed for Marinella. But then . . . You know where, just when you reach the seafront, there's a petrol station on the right that's no longer in use?'

'Of course.'

'Well, a short way past it, there's an unmade road that goes up the hill. That's where he turned. I know that road because it leads up to some houses, including one that I've been to a few times. I had to keep fairly close behind his car because the road intersects with quite a few others that lead to the different houses. If he'd turned off the main road, it would have been hard to keep following him. But in fact he stopped in front of the fourth house on the right, got out, opened the gate, and went in.'

'And what did you do?'

'I continued on.'

'You passed behind him?'

'Yes, but he turned around.'

'Damn!'

'Calm down. There's no way he could have recognized me. I've only had my Micra for a week.'

'Yes, but you yourself are very—'

'Recognizable? Even with sunglasses and a great big hat à la Greta Garbo?'

'Let's hope you're right. Go on.'

'A little bit later I came back, but with the engine

turned off. Mimì's car was in the garden. He'd gone inside.'

'Did you wait for the woman to arrive?'

'Of course. Until half an hour ago. I never saw her arrive.'

'So what does it mean?'

'Look, Salvo, when I drove past the house the first time, I swear I saw the light on inside. There was someone there waiting for him.'

'You mean the woman lives there?'

'Not necessarily. Mimì left his car in the garden. He didn't put it in a little garage next to the house, maybe because the woman had already put her own car in it when she got there.'

'But, Ingrid, the garage might have the woman's car in it not because she got there shortly before Mimì, but because she lives there.'

'That's also possible. At any rate, Mimì didn't knock or ring when he arrived. He opened the gate with a key he already had.'

'Why didn't you wait a little longer?'

'Because too many people were starting to pass by.'

'Thanks,' said Montalbano.

'Thanks? That's all?' asked Ingrid.

'Thanks, and that's all,' said Montalbano.

✻

Before leaving the house just before nine o'clock, the inspector phoned the Anti-Mafia Commission's Monte-lusa office.

'Hello, Musante? Montalbano here.'

'My dear! What a pleasure to hear from you! What can I do for you?'

'Could I drop by this morning? There's something I wanted to talk to you about, it shouldn't take long.'

'Could you come in about an hour? I've got a meeting afterwards that—'

'Thanks, see you in a bit.'

He got in his car, and when he was at the abandoned petrol station, he did an extremely slow U-turn that unleashed the worst murderous instincts in the drivers behind him. He turned onto the unmade road, and after a short stretch passed by the fourth house. Windows shuttered, garage door down. The gate, however, was open because an old man was working in the garden, which was well tended. The inspector stopped, parked the car, got out, and started looking at the house.

'Looking for someone?' asked the old man.

'Yes. A Mr Casanova, who's supposed to live here.'

'Afraid not, sir. You're mistaken. Nobody lives here.'

'But who owns the house?'

'Mr Pecorini. But he only comes here in summer.'

'Where can I find this Mr Pecorini?'

'He's in Catania. Works at the port, at customs.'

He got back in the car and headed for the station. If he got to Montelusa five minutes late, too bad. He parked in the station car park but remained in the car, pressed his hand on the horn and did not let up until Catarella appeared in the doorway.

Seeing the inspector in his car, he came running up.

'Whattizzit, Chief? Whass wrong?'

'Fazio around?'

'Yessir.'

'Call him.'

Fazio arrived like a bat out of hell.

'Fazio, get moving, fast. I want to know everything there is to know about a certain Pecorini who works at customs in the port of Catania.'

'Should I proceed with caution, Chief?'

'Yeah, it's probably better if you do.'

*

The local headquarters of the national Anti-Mafia Commission consisted of four offices on the fifth floor of the Montelusa Central Police building. As the lift was, as usual, out of order, Montalbano started climbing the stairs. Looking up when he'd reached the third floor, he saw Dr Lattes descending. To avoid the usual hassle of answering his idiotic questions about the family, he took a handkerchief out of his pocket and buried his face in it, heaving his shoulders as if he were weeping uncontrollably. Dr Lattes recoiled against the wall and let him pass, not daring to say a word.

*

'Want some coffee?' asked Musante.

'No, thanks,' said Montalbano.

He didn't trust what passed for coffee in law-enforcement offices.

'So, tell me everything.'

'Well, Musante, I believe I have a murder on my hands that looks like the work of the Mafia.'

'Stop right there. Answer me a question. In what form are you going to say what you are about to say to me?'

'In loose hendecasyllables.'

'C'mon, Montalbano, be serious.'

'Sorry, but I didn't understand your question.'

'I meant, are you telling me this officially or unofficially?'

'What difference does it make?'

'If it's official, then I have to write up a transcript; if it's unofficial, I have to have a witness present.'

'I see.'

Apparently they didn't take any chances at the Anti-Mafia Commission. Given the ties between the Mafia and the upper echelons of business, industry, and government, it was best to cover one's back and proceed with caution.

'Since you're a friend, I'll give you a choice of witnesses. Gullotta or Campana?'

'Gullotta.'

The inspector knew him well and liked him.

Musante went out and returned a few minutes later with Gullotta, who smiled as he shook Montalbano's hand. It was clear he was happy to see him.

'You can go on now,' said Musante.

'I'm referring to the unknown man we found dismembered in a rubbish bag. Have you heard about it?'

'Yes,' said Musante and Gullotta in chorus.

'Do you know how he was killed?'

'No,' said the chorus.

'With a bullet to the base of the skull.'

'Ah!' exclaimed the chorus.

At that moment there was a knock at the door.

'Come in!' said the chorus in chorus.

A mustachioed man of about fifty came in, looked at Montalbano, then looked at Musante and signalled to him that he wanted to tell him something. Musante stood up, the man whispered something to him in his ear and then left. Musante then gestured to Gullotta, who got up and went over to him. Musante whispered into Gullotta's ear, and they both turned and looked at Montalbano. Then they looked at each other and sat back down.

'If that was a mime scene, I didn't get it,' said Montalbano.

'Go on,' Musante said in a serious tone.

'The fact of the shot to the base of the skull would already be one indication,' the inspector resumed. 'But there's more. Are you familiar with the Gospel according to St Matthew?'

'What?!' said Gullotta, thrown for a loop.

Musante, for his part, bent down towards Montalbano, laid a hand on his knee, and asked him lovingly: 'Are you sure you're all right?'

'Of course I'm all right.'

'You're not upset?'

'Not at all!'

'Well, then why, just a few minutes ago, were you crying uncontrollably in the stairwell?'

So that's what the man with the moustache had come in to tell him! Montalbano felt lost. Now how was he going to explain the whole complicated affair to these two, who were looking at him with a combination of concern and suspicion? He was hoist with his own petard. He gave a sort of forced smile, took on (he knew not from where) a nonchalant air, and said:

'Oh, that? It's Dr Lattes's fault. He—'

'Did he scold you or something? Raise his voice at you?' asked Musante, bemused.

'Reprimand you?' Gullotta laid it on.

Was it possible neither of them could speak for himself? No, it wasn't possible.

Laurel and Hardy. A comic duo.

'No, no, the whole thing is because, after I told him my wife had run away with an illegal immigrant, I—'

'But you're not married!' Musante, alarmed, reminded him.

'Or maybe you got married and never told us?' Gullotta hypothesized.

'No, no, of course I'm not married. But, you see, since, afterwards, I told him my wife had returned for the children—'

'You have children?' Gullotta asked him, amazed.

'How old are they?' Musante followed.

'No, no . . .'

He lost heart. He couldn't go on. Words failed him. He buried his face in his hands.

'You're not going to start crying again in here?!' Musante asked him, alarmed.

'Come on, have faith. There's a solution to everything,' said Gullotta.

How to explain? Start yelling? Break both their noses? Pull out his pistol and force them to listen? They would think him stark raving mad. He tried to remain calm, and in the effort, he started sweating.

'Could you both do me a favour and just listen to me for five minutes?'

'Of course, of course,' the chorus resumed.

'The story that I was crying is true, though I wasn't really crying.'

'Of course, of course.'

It was hopeless. By now they were convinced he was

raving and were treating him gingerly, humouring him and pretending they agreed with him, the way one does with the insane so they won't go berserk.

'I swear I'm fine,' said the inspector. 'I just want you to bear with me and pay attention.'

'Of course, of course.'

He told them the whole story, from the reading of the Camilleri book to his call to Dr Pasquano. When he had finished, a thoughtful silence descended. But he had the impression that Musante and Gullotta had changed their minds and no longer considered him quite so crazy.

'Do you find there's method in my madness?' asked Montalbano.

'Well . . .' said Gullotta, not catching his Shakespearian allusion.

'In short, why did you come here and tell us all this?' asked Musante.

Montalbano looked at him, stunned.

'Because that dead body most assuredly belongs to a Mafioso who was murdered by his colleagues. Or are you only interested in living Mafiosi?'

Musante and Gullotta exchanged a glance.

'No,' said Gullotta. 'We're always interested, whether they're dead or alive. From what I can gather, you seem to want to unload the case on us.'

'Since you're a bit overwrought, you want to wash your hands of it,' Musante said in an understanding tone.

Jesus, what a pain!

'Look, I'm not trying to unload anything, and I'm not overwrought.'

'No? Then what *are* you trying to do?'

'Yes, *what*, exactly?' Gullotta chimed in, introducing a notable variant into the repertoire.

'Unless I am mistaken, all Mafia investigations in this jurisdiction belong to you, do they not?'

'Yes, of course they do,' said Musante. 'But only when we are certain that the Mafia are indeed implicated.'

'One hundred per cent certain,' said Gullotta.

'So I didn't convince you?'

'Yes, you did, in part, and verbally. But we can't very well go to our superiors saying that you became firmly convinced reading some silly novel like Camilleri's . . .'

'And the Gospel according to Matthew,' Gullotta concluded.

'How old are you?' Montalbano asked them.

'I'm forty-two,' said Musante.

'And I'm forty-four,' said Gullotta.

'You're too young,' Montalbano observed.

'What do you mean?'

They were talking in chorus again.

'I mean you've become accustomed to today's Mafia and no longer understand a thing about semiology.'

'Semiology? I've never even—' Gullotta began doubtfully.

'You see, Montalbano,' Musante interrupted him, 'if you had actually identified the body, and we were certain that it belonged to a Mafioso, then—'

'I get it,' said the inspector. 'You want your lunch served to you on fine china.'

In perfect sync, the chorus threw their hands in the air to express their regret.

Montalbano stood up; the chorus stood up.

'Can I ask you something?'

'If we can be of help...'

'As far as you know, was there any notable activity in the Vigàta-area Mafia about two months ago?'

Montalbano realized that these words had got the attention of the two-man chorus. They had straightened themselves up from the relaxed posture of farewell they had assumed.

'Why?' the chorus asked warily.

Damned if he was going to tell them now that the dismembered stranger's death dated from about two months ago.

'Oh, I dunno, just wondering...'

'No, there hasn't been anything,' said Musante.

'Nothing at all,' Gullotta confirmed.

Apparently, when they had to lie, they became soloists. It was clear they had no intention whatsoever to let a borderline madman like him in on a secret investigation.

They said goodbye.

'Take care of yourself,' Gullotta suggested.

'Take a few days off,' Musante advised.

*

So something had definitely happened two months earlier. Something the Anti-Mafia Commission was keeping hidden because the investigation was still ongoing.

When he got to the station he called Fazio and told him of his conversation with Musante and Gullotta. He did not tell him, of course, that they thought he was crazy.

'Have you got any friends at Anti-Mafia?'

'Sure, Chief. Morici.'

'Is he about fifty, with a moustache?' asked Montalbano, alarmed.

'No.'

'Could you talk to him?'

'What do you want me to say?'

'Ask him if he knows what happened two months ago, which Musante and Gullotta didn't want to tell me.'

'I can try, Chief, but . . .'

'But what?'

'Morici and I may be friends, but he's a man of few words. The man's like a statue. He doesn't even sweat.'

'Well, try to make him sweat a little. Have you started working on Pecorini?'

'Yes, sir. I've started and I've even finished. The response was negative.'

'Meaning?'

'He doesn't work at customs in Catania and never has. Nobody with that name has.'

'Ah, I see. Maybe the person who gave me this information didn't mean "customs" as in "customs office", but was simply referring to that part of town. People do talk that way, sometimes.'

'So where am I supposed to find him now, this Pecorini?'

Wasn't it possible that Mimì went through an agency to rent that house?

'Listen, how many estate agents are there in Vigàta?'

Fazio did a quick mental tally.

'Five and a half, Chief.'

'What do you mean by "a half"?'

'There's one that also sells cars.'

'See if Pecorini used one of them to rent a house.'

'To rent it himself or to rent it out to others?'

'To rent it out. He owns the house. And if you have any luck, get them to tell you where he works, or at least where he lives. He must have an address and phone number with the agency.'

'Do you know the address of the house?'

'No.'

It was best not to give Fazio too much information. He was liable to discover that Mimì was renting it.

*

That afternoon, as he was coming back into the station, he nearly collided with Mimì Augello, who was coming out in a hurry.

'Greetings, Mimì.'

'Greetings,' Mimì replied brusquely.

Montalbano turned around to look at him as he headed through the car park towards his car. Mimì seemed to be walking with his back slightly hunched.

At that very moment another car parked right beside Mimì's, and from it emerged a woman of more than considerable beauty.

But Augello didn't consider her at all. He didn't even look at her, in fact, but only started his car and left.

How he had changed! Once upon a time, Mimì would most certainly have tried to strike up a conversation and make friends with a woman like that.

NINE

Five minutes after the inspector had sat down at his desk, the door flew open and slammed against the wall with such force that it frightened Catarella himself, the author of what should have been a simple knock.

'Man, what a crash! Even scared me m'self, Chief! Ahhh, Chief! What a woman!'

'Where?'

'Right 'ere, Chief. Inna waitin' room. Says 'er name's Dolorosa. I say it oughta be Amorosa! Says she wants a talk t'yiz poissonally in poisson. Jesus, whatta woman! Ya gotta have eyes t'see this one!'

She must be the woman the inspector saw get out of the car. A woman who puts even Catarella in a state like that, and Mimì doesn't deign to give her a glance? Poor Mimì! He was in a really bad way!

'Send her in.'

*

She didn't seem real. She was stunning, about thirty, dark and very tall, with long hair falling over her shoulders, big, deep eyes, a broad mouth, full lips siliconized not by a surgeon but by Mother Nature herself, perfect teeth for eating living flesh, and big hoop earrings, like a gypsy. Also gypsy-like were her skirt and a blouse that swelled with two international-tournament-size bowling balls.

She didn't seem real, but she was. Christ, was she real.

Montalbano had the impression he'd already met her somewhere, but then realized that it was because she looked like a Mexican movie actress from the Fifties he'd seen in a recent retrospective.

When she entered, the office filled with a faint scent of cinnamon.

But it wasn't perfume that gave off that scent, the inspector thought. It was her skin. As she held out her hand to him, Montalbano noticed that she had extremely long fingers, disproportionately long, fascinating and dangerous.

They sat down, she in front, he behind the desk. The woman had a serious, worried air about her.

'What can I do for you, signora . . . ?'

'My name is Dolores Alfano.'

Montalbano sprang up towards the ceiling, and on his way back down, his left buttock landed on the edge of the chair and he very nearly disappeared behind the desk. Dolores Alfano seemed not to notice.

ANDREA CAMILLERI

So here, at last, personally in person, was the mysterious woman Fabio Giacchetti had talked to him about, the woman who, returning from an amorous tryst, nearly got run over by someone, perhaps on purpose.

'Alfano, however, is my husband Giovanni's surname,' she continued. 'My maiden name is Gutierrez.'

'Are you Spanish?'

'No, Colombian. But I've been living in Vigàta for years, at Via Guttuso, 12.'

'So, what can I do for you, signora?' Montalbano repeated.

'My husband is away at sea, sailing on a container ship as a first mate. We stay in touch through letters and postcards. Before leaving, he always gives me a list of his ports of call with arrival and departure dates, so he can receive my letters when he goes ashore. We also sometimes call each other with our satellite phones, but pretty rarely.'

'Has something happened?'

'What's happened is that Giovanni embarked a few months ago on a rather long voyage, and after three weeks had gone by, he still hadn't written or phoned me. This had never happened before. So I got worried and called him. He told me he was in good health and had been very busy.'

Montalbano was spellbound as he listened to her. She had a bedroom voice. There was no other way to define it. She might say only 'hello', and immediately one

132

imagined rumpled blankets, pillows on the floor, and sweat-dampened sheets that smelled like cinnamon.

And the Spanish accent that came out when she spoke at length was like a spicy condiment.

'... a postcard from him,' said Dolores.

Lost in her voice, Montalbano had become distracted, his mind indeed on unmade beds and torrid nights, with perhaps some Spanish guitars playing in the background...

'I'm sorry, what did you say?' he said.

'I said that the day before yesterday, I got a postcard from him.'

'Good. So now you've been reassured.'

The woman did not reply, but pulled a picture postcard out of her purse and handed it to the inspector.

It showed the port of a town that Montalbano had never heard of. The stamp was Argentinian. On the back was written: *Doing great. How about you? Kisses, Giovanni.*

You couldn't very well say the sea captain was an expansive sort. Still, it was better than nothing. Montalbano looked up at Dolores Alfano.

'I don't think he wrote it himself,' she said. 'The signature looks different to me.'

She took four other postcards out of her purse and passed them to Montalbano.

'Compare it with these, which he sent me last year.'

There was no need to resort to a handwriting expert. It was glaringly obvious that the handwriting of the last postcard was fake. And falsified, above all, rather carelessly. The old postcards also had a different tone:

I love you so much

Think of you always

I miss you

I kiss you all over

'This last postcard I received,' Dolores continued, 'brought back the strange impression I had after calling him on the phone.'

'Which was?'

'That it wasn't him at the other end. His voice was different. As if he had a cold. But at the time I convinced myself that it was because of the distortion of the phone. Now I'm no longer so sure.'

'And what do you think I should do?'

'Well ... I don't really know.'

'It's a bit of a problem, signora. The last postcard wasn't written by him, you're right about that. But that might also mean your husband didn't board the ship for any number of reasons and then had a friend write to you and send it so you wouldn't get worried.'

Dolores shook her head.

'In that case, he could have telephoned me.'

'True. Why didn't *you* call him?'

'I did. As soon as I received the card. And I called him twice after that. I even tried again before coming here. But his telephone is always turned off, nobody answers.'

'I understand your concern, signora, but...'

'So you can't do anything?'

'No, I can't. Because, you see, the way things are today, you aren't even in a position to file a missing person's report. Who's to say whether the situation isn't other than what you say it is?'

'But what could the situation be, in that case?'

'Well, I dunno, for example . . .' Montalbano started walking on eggshells. 'Mind you, this is only a conjecture, but maybe your husband met somebody . . . You know what I mean? . . . Somebody who—'

'My husband loves me.'

She said it serenely, almost without intonation. Then she took an envelope out of her purse and withdrew the letter that was inside it.

'This is a letter he sent me four months ago. Please read it.'

> ... *not a night goes by that I don't dream of being inside you*
> *... I hear again the things you say when you are reaching*
> *orgasm ... and immediately you want to start all over again*
> *... when your tongue ...*

Montalbano blushed, decided he'd seen enough, and gave the letter back to her.

Maybe it was just his imagination, but he thought he saw, deep inside the woman's deep dark eyes, gone as fast as it had appeared, a flash of . . . irony? Amusement?

'The last time he was here, how did your husband behave?'

'With me? The same as always.'

'Listen, signora, all I can do at this point is give you some, er, personal advice. Do you know the name of the ship on which your husband is embarked?'

'Yes, the *Ruy Barbosa*.'

'Then get in touch with the shipping agents. Are they Italian?'

'No. Stevenson & Guerra are Brazilian.'

'Do they have a representative in Italy?'

'Of course, in Naples. His name is Pasquale Camera.'

'Have you got an address and telephone number for this Pasquale Camera?'

'Yes, I've got them here.'

She took a piece of paper out of her purse and held it out to Montalbano.

'No, don't give it to me. It's you who has to call for the information.'

'No, I can't,' Dolores said decisively.

'Why not?'

'Because I don't want my husband to think that I . . . No, I'd rather not. Please, you do it.'

'Me? But, signora, as a police inspector I ca—'

'Just say you're a friend of Giovanni's and you're worried because you've had no news of him for a while.'

'Look, signora, I—'

Dolores leaned forward. Montalbano was resting his arms on the desktop. The woman laid her hands, hot as if with fever, on top of Montalbano's, her long fingers snaking inside the cuffs of his shirt, first caressing his skin, then clutching his wrists.

'Help me,' she said.

'All ... all right,' said Montalbano.

They stood up. The inspector went to open the door for her and saw that half the police department was in the waiting room, all feigning indifference.

Apparently Catarella had passed the word about Dolores's beauty.

*

Once alone, the inspector took off his jacket, unbuttoned his cuffs, and pulled up his sleeves.

Dolores's fingernails had left marks on his skin. She had branded him. His skin burned a little. He sniffed his arms, which smelled slightly of cinnamon. Wasn't it best to settle the matter at once? And get this black leopardess out of his hair? The less he saw of her, the better.

'Catarella! Ring this number in Naples for me. But don't tell them you're calling for the police.'

Times table for eigh——. A woman picked up at once.

'Camera Shipping Agency. May I help you?'

'Davide Maraschi here. I'd like to speak to Mr Camera.'

ANDREA CAMILLERI

'Please hold.'

A recording of a song in keeping with the setting began: *O sole mio.*

'Could you please hold?' the woman cut in. 'Mr Camera is on another line.'

A new song: *Fenesta ca lucive.*

'Could you hold just a minute longer?'

New song: *Guapparia.*

The inspector liked Neapolitan songs, but he was starting to wish they would play some rock. Discouraged and worried he was going to have to sing along with the entire repertoire of the Piedigrotta Festival, he was about to hang up when a man's voice cut in:

'Hello, this is Camera. What can I do for you?'

What the hell did he tell the secretary his name was? He remembered Davide, but not the surname, except for the fact that it ended in *—schi.*

'I'm Davide Verzaschi.'

'How may I help you?'

'I'll take only a few minutes of your time, as I can see you're very busy. You represent Stevenson & Guerra, correct?'

'Among others.'

'Good. Listen, I urgently need to get in touch with someone presently on board the *Ruy Barbosa.* Would you be so kind as to explain to me how I might go about this?'

'How do you intend to get in touch with this person?'

'I've ruled out carrier pigeons and smoke signals.'

'I don't understand,' said Camera.

But why did he always have to make wisecracks? The agent might hang up, and that would be the end of that.

'I don't know, in writing or by telephone.'

'If you have a satellite phone, you only have to dial the number.'

'I have, but nobody answers.'

'I see. Wait just a minute while I check the computer ... Here we are. The *Ruy Barbosa* will be calling at Lisbon in exactly eight days. So you can write a letter. I can even give you the address of the Portuguese representative and—'

'Isn't there a quicker way? I have some bad news to tell him. His aunt Adelaide has died; she was like a mother to him.'

The pause that followed meant that Mr Camera was torn between duty and pity. And the latter won.

'Look, I'll make an exception, given the gravity and urgency of the matter. I'll give you the mobile-phone number of the first mate, who is also the ship's purser. Write this down.'

So how was he going to wiggle out of this now? The first mate of the *Ruy Barbosa* was the person he was looking for! He couldn't think of a single way to get out the predicament.

'The first mate,' Mr Camera continued, 'is named Couto Ribeiro, and his number is—'

What was he saying?

'I'm sorry, but isn't the first mate Giovanni Alfano?'

There was a sudden silence at the other end.

And Montalbano was seized by the same sense of panic that always came over him when the line got cut off as he was speaking on the telephone. It was as if he'd been rocketed into the icy loneliness of outer space. He started yelling desperately.

'Hello? Helllloooo?'

'No need to shout. Are you a relative of Alfano's?'

'No, we're friends, former schoolmates, and . . .'

'Where are you calling from?'

'From . . . from Brindisi.'

'So you're not in Vigàta.'

Elementary, my dear Watson.

'How long has it been since you last saw Alfano?' the man continued.

What the hell had got into Camera? What were all these questions? His tone was brusque, almost angry.

'Well . . . it's probably been a little over two months . . . He told me his next job would be aboard the *Ruy Barbosa*, as first mate. Which is why I'm surprised . . . What happened?'

'What happened is that he never turned up to board the ship. I had to look for a substitute at the very last minute, and it wasn't easy. Your friend got me into trouble, a great deal of trouble, in fact.'

'Have you heard from him since?'

'Three days later he sent me a note saying he'd found something better. Listen, if you get hold of him, tell him that Camera's going to kick his arse all the way to Sardinia if he sees him. So, what are we going to do, Mr...'

'Falaschi.'

'. . . are you going to take down Couto Ribeiro's number or not?'

'Please go ahead.'

'Oh, no you don't! Get clever with me, will you? First you must clarify something for me, my dear Mr Panaschi. If you knew Alfano was aboard the *Ruy Barbosa*, why didn't you phone him instead of me?'

Montalbano hung up.

*

The inspector's first thought was that Giovanni Alfano had bolted on the sly from the domestic hearth, to use an expression dear to Dr Lattes. Sailing, sailing, day in, day out, putting into port after port, he must certainly have met another woman in some far-away town. Maybe a platinum Vikingess who smelled of soap and water, after tiring of dark, cinnamon-flavoured Colombian flesh.

By now he was probably cruising blissfully through the fjords of the North Sea. With a fond farewell and best wishes. Who was ever going to track him down?

He'd planned his scheme pretty well, had Mr Captain of the High Seas.

He'd failed to show up for embarkation, sent Camera a note with the bogus story that he'd found a better deal somewhere else, given his mobile phone to a friend, saying that if his wife called he should pretend he's him, and asked him to send Dolores a phony postcard two months down the line. And so he'd gained a good leg-up before his wife even realized he'd fled the coop and started her futile search.

What to do now?

Go at once to Via Guttuso 12, knock on the door, and inform the leopardess that she'd become a widow, if only by forfeit?

How do leopardesses react when they learn their leopard has left them? Do they scratch? Do they bite? And what if, by chance, she started crying, threw herself into his arms, and wanted to be comforted?

No, it was a rather dangerous idea.

Perhaps it was best to phone her.

But aren't there certain things you just can't say over the telephone? Montalbano was certain that once he got to the heart of the matter, he would get tongue-tied. No, it was safer to write her a note. And advise her, before filing a missing person's report, to talk to the people at *Missing*, the TV programme where they look for, and often find, missing persons before the police even get started.

But wasn't it perhaps better to put it all off till tomorrow?

One day more or less wasn't going to make any difference. On the contrary. This way, Signora Dolores would actually gain an extra night of peace.

Till tomorrow, he concluded, till tomorrow.

*

He was about to leave his office and head home when Fazio came in. From the face he was wearing it was clear he had something big up his sleeve. He was about to open his mouth when he noticed the scratches on the inspector's forearms and changed expression.

'Wha'?? How'd you scratch yourself like that? Have you disinfected them?'

'I didn't scratch myself,' said Montalbano, annoyed, rolling down his shirtsleeves. 'And there's no need to disinfect them.'

'So how'd you get them, then?'

'Jesus! I'll tell you later. Talk to me.'

'So. First of all, Pecorini didn't use any agency to rent out his house. I called them all. However, a certain Mr Maiorca, owner of one of the agencies, when he heard me mention Pecorini over the telephone, said, "Who, the butcher?" "Do you know him?" I asked. And he said, "Yes." So I went and talked to him in person.'

He pulled out a little piece of paper from which he was about to read something, but a murderous glance from Montalbano stopped him dead.

'OK, OK, Chief, no vital statistics. Just the bare

essentials. The Pecorini of interest to us is a fifty-year-old from Vigàta, first name Arturo, who lived in Vigàta until two years ago and worked as a butcher. Then he moved to Catania where he opened an enormous butcher's shop at the port, near the customs house. Fits the bill, no?'

'Seems to. Is the summer house the only thing he kept in Vigàta?'

'No. He's got another house, in town, that had always been his main residence, in Via Pippo Rizzo.'

'Do you know where that street is?'

'Yeah, in that same rich neighbourhood I said I didn't like. It runs parallel to Via Guttuso.'

'I see. And he only comes back here in the summer?'

'Who ever said that? He kept his butcher's shop here, and got his brother, Ignazio, to look after it. And he comes here every Saturday to see how the business is going.'

Maybe – thought Montalbano – Mimì got to know the butcher from buying meat at his shop and found out, or already knew, that Pecorini had an empty house for rent. That might explain it.

'Did you also talk with your friend at the Anti-Mafia Commission, Morici?'

'I did. We're meeting tomorrow morning at nine in a bar in Montelusa. Now will you tell me how you got those scratches?'

'Dolores Alfano did it.'

Fazio was taken aback.

'Is she as beautiful as they say?'

'Very beautiful.'

'She came here?'

'Yes.'

'Did she come to report the person who tried to run her over?'

'The subject never even came up.'

'Then what did she want?'

Montalbano had to explain the whole matter to him, including the disappearance of Giovanni Alfano.

'And how did she scratch you?'

A little embarrassed, Montalbano explained.

'Be careful, Chief. That lady bites.'

TEN

He had just finished savouring the aubergine *parmigiana* when Livia called.

'I've been on the phone for the last half-hour to Beba. She's desperate and can't stop crying.'

'But why?'

'Because Mimì is treating her very badly. He screams and yells and it's not at all clear what he wants. This morning he made a terrible scene. Beba thinks these night-time stake-outs are wearing him out.'

'Did you tell her they'll be over soon?'

'Yes, but, in the meantime . . . Poor Beba . . . But tell me something, Salvo. Has Mimì done any stake-outs like these in the past?'

'Sure, dozens.'

'And he's never reacted this way before?'

'Never.'

'So, why is it that now . . . Bah! Couldn't it be that something else is going on in his life?'

An alarm bell went off in the inspector's head.

'Like what?'

'I dunno . . . Maybe he's fallen in love with someone else . . . Mimì used to fall in love so easily . . . Maybe, between the exhaustion from his stake-outs and the uneasiness he feels around Beba . . .'

For heaven's sake, that idea wasn't supposed to even graze Livia's consciousness! It could compromise everything!

'I'm sorry, Livia, but when could he have met this other woman? He hasn't got the time. Think about it. At the moment, he spends his nights on stake-outs or at home, and during the day he's at the office . . .'

'You're right. But why suddenly all these stake-outs, and all on Mimì's shoulders?'

Shit! Livia was becoming dangerous. Guided by her feminine sense of smell, she was getting close to the truth. There were two ways to throw her off the scent: either start yelling like a madman that the rise in crime was not his fault, or else try to reason calmly. If he did the former, the conversation would end in disgust, and Livia would simply harden her position; whereas, with the latter, maybe . . .

'Well, the situation here has practically become a state of emergency, you know . . . There's a band of fugitives roaming the countryside . . . We've already caught one person, thanks, in fact, to Mimì. And it's not true that it's all on Mimì's shoulders. He's been going out every other night, more or less. On his nights off, he's replaced by someone else.'

All lies. But Livia seemed to have been convinced.

*

Before going to bed, he turned on the television. The purse-lipped mouth of Pippo Ragonese's chicken-arse face was saying something related to him.

'. . . and I am certainly not referring to possible developments in the investigation of the dismembered murder victim found in the area called 'u critaru. To be perfectly frank, I am, unfortunately, quite certain that that case will eventually be closed without the killer's or the victim's names ever having been discovered. No, I am referring to what might happen later, in the investigation of some future crime of considerable gravity. Will the Vigàta Police be able to work as a unit on a complex case, without internal misunderstandings that could undermine their solidarity? This, in fact, is our fear. And you can count on my coming back to this subject in the very near future.'

As they entered one ear and went out the other, those words disturbed the inspector greatly. Internal misunderstandings. Clearly Ragonese had got wind, in one way or another, of what was happening in the department because of Mimì. He knew only half the story. And it was absolutely crucial to stop him before he knew all of it. But how? The inspector would have to think about this.

*

The following morning he got dressed up, even putting on a tie. It didn't seem right to go see Dolores Alfano dressed casually, having, as he did, to give her news which, no matter how you looked at it, was bad.

But since it was still too early – a few minutes to nine – to pay her a call, the inspector dropped by the station first.

'Ahh, Chief, Chief! Y'look so fancy when y'get dressed up all fancy!' Catarella commented in admiration.

'Anyone here?'

'Yessir, Fazio.'

'Send him to me.'

Fazio came in, looked at him, and asked: 'You on your way to see Signora Alfano?'

'Yeah, in a little bit. And you're coming too.'

Fazio was unprepared for this.

'But . . . why? Aren't you enough?'

'Didn't you say yourself that she bites? If you're there too, you might help keep her still and prevent her from biting me.'

'Whatever you say, Chief. Meanwhile, I've already seen Morici.'

'So soon?'

'Yeah, Chief. Yesterday he was told he had to go to Palermo for a week, and so he phoned me and moved the appointment to seven o'clock this morning.'

'What did he tell you?'

'Well, something strange. He said they'd received a tip that turned out to be a red herring.'

'Meaning?'

'About two months ago, they received an anonymous letter.'

'Just for a change!'

'But this one seemed different, like it might contain a grain of truth.'

'What did it say?'

'That Don Balduccio Sinagra had had somebody killed.'

'Don Balduccio? He's over ninety years old! Hasn't he retired from the family business?'

'I don't know what to tell you, Chief. That's what the letter said. It explained that Don Balduccio intervened in that particular instance because he felt personally offended.'

'I see. And who was it that offended him and who he put the hit on?'

'The letter didn't give his name. But it did say he was a courier who had sold some merchandise instead of delivering it.'

'And then?'

'The Anti-Mafia people got moving right away. If they could get their hands on even a little proof, it would be a major coup. And they didn't ask for any help from Narcotics – you know how these things are. But if they had, they would have saved themselves some time.'

'Why?'

'After four frantic days of investigation, Inspector Musante happened to run into Inspector Ballerini from Narcotics, who in the course of the conversation told him that Don Balduccio Sinagra was in a coma in a Palermo clinic. And so they decided that Balduccio couldn't have given the order to have anyone killed. And, at any rate, they hadn't found anything, not even the courier's corpse.'

'And what was their conclusion?'

'That someone had taken them for a ride, Chief.'

'Or someone wanted to make trouble for Don Balduccio, not knowing he was in a coma.'

*

'... and so, to conclude, your husband never boarded the *Ruy Barbosa*.'

Dolores Alfano froze like a statue.

She was standing in front of Montalbano and Fazio, who were sitting in two armchairs in her living room, and about to serve them coffee. Her left arm remained raised in mid-air, perhaps to brush her hair back, while her right arm reached downwards.

For a split second, the inspector felt as if he was looking at a sugar-doll of a dancing girl, which were almost always Spanish dancers. Even the scent of cinnamon, which immediately grew stronger, added to this impression. He felt a terrible desire to stick out his tongue and lick her neck so he could taste her skin, which must surely be sweet.

The lady then came back to life. Saying nothing, she completed the movements she had begun. She brushed the hair away from her eyes, bent forward to pour the coffee into the two cups with a steady hand, asked them how much sugar they took, put this in the cups, which she then handed them, and sat down on the sofa.

Montalbano was watching her. She hadn't lost colour, and showed no surprise or agitation at the news. The only outward sign was a deep, straight furrow cutting horizontally across her brow. She waited until the two men had finished their coffee before she spoke.

'You're not joking, are you?'

No drama in her tone, no cracking in her voice from pent-up tears. A simple, flat question.

'No, unfortunately,' said Montalbano.

'What do you think could have happened to him?' she asked in the same tone, as if she were talking about someone without the slightest connection to her.

Sugar-doll? She was a woman of marble and steel, was Signora Dolores! A contradictory woman, though: able to control herself, as she was at this moment, but also liable to abandon herself to acts of passion, such as when she scratched his arm.

'Well, the most likely scenario is a voluntary dis-appearance.'

'Why do you say that?'

'Because Mr Camera told me that a few days after not showing up for boarding, your husband sent him a note saying he'd found a better offer.'

'But that could be a forgery, like the postcard I received the other day,' Dolores replied readily.

Intelligent woman, no doubt about it, whose brain still functioned in spite of the blow she'd just received.

'That's precisely why I would like to get my hands on that note, provided Camera still has it.'

'Why don't you try?'

'Before I can make any moves, I need a formal missing-persons declaration from you.'

'All right, then, I'll do that. Should I come with you?'

'There's no need. Fazio can take down your declar-ation right here, after I leave. I would, however, like to ask you a few more things.'

'So would I.'

'All right, then, after you.'

'But first, please, if you have other questions to ask me, come and sit on the sofa beside me. I can't . . .'

For a millionth of a second, Fazio's and Montalbano's eyes met. Then Montalbano did as asked.

'Is that better?' he said, settling in.

'Yes, thank you.'

'Have you got a recent photo of your husband?'

'As many as you like. There are even some we took a few days before he left. I'd gone along with him to say goodbye to a distant relative of his...'

'All right, you can show me them later, and I'll select one to take with me. But now I have to ask you something I already asked you yesterday, which I'm sure will be unpleasant for you. I'm sorry, but...'

Dolores raised a hand and placed it on Montalbano's knee. It was hot and trembling ever so lightly. Apparently only now was what the inspector had told her beginning to sink in. And it was becoming harder for her to control herself.

'From the letter you kindly showed me yesterday, it was clear that your relationship with your husband was very... well, very intense. Would you say that's true?'

Fazio suddenly leaned forward, closer to the notebook on his leg, and pretended to take notes.

'Yes. Very intense,' said Dolores.

'And during your husband's last stay here, would you say — and I want you to think this over very carefully — would you say that this ... this intensity had perhaps diminished a little? Was there maybe a cooling, however minor, that might ... What I mean is, was anything at all different from the other times he...'

She squeezed his knee tight. And the heat of her hand travelled straight as an arrow from that point and up his thigh just enough to reach a rather delicate spot in the inspector's anatomy. He gave a start, barely able to contain himself.

'Something was very different,' she said so softly that Fazio had to lean forward to hear her.

'But the last time we spoke, you said the opposite,' the inspector was quick to point out.

'Well ... because Giovanni *was* ... different ... which isn't really the right word, not in the sense that you think ...'

'How, then?'

But why didn't she take her damn hand off his knee?

'In fact, he had become . . . it was like he was starving. Nothing was ever enough. Two or three times, when we had just finished eating, he couldn't even wait for me to get to the bedroom . . . And he would ask me to do things which before ...'

Having become suddenly short-sighted, Fazio raised his notebook directly in front of his eyes, to hide his blushing face. Dolores's palm, for its part, had started sweating at the memory of those recent connubial exploits, to the point that Montalbano could feel the dampness through the fabric of his trousers.

'Perhaps if I give you a few details, you'll better understand the degree—'

'No! No details!' Montalbano nearly yelled, suddenly standing up.

He couldn't stand it any longer. That hand was driving him out of his wits.

She looked at him as if baffled. Was it possible she had no idea of the effect her hand and voice had on a man?

'All right, signora,' Montalbano continued. 'Let's consider this chapter closed. Tell me, does your husband have any enemies?'

'Inspector, all I know about my husband's life is what he chooses to tell me, in person or in writing. He's certainly never mentioned anything about enemies. It's true he's talked a few times about some arguments he'd had with other officers or crew members, but those were all things of no importance.'

'What about here in Vigàta?'

'But by now Giovanni has very few friends in Vigàta! He moved to Colombia with his parents when he was still very young, did his studies there and then, when his father died, a relative from Vigàta helped him out until he sailed for the first time as a professional. He's lived more abroad than here.'

'Do you know the names and addresses of any of these friends?'

'Of course.'

'You can give them to Fazio later. When Giovanni's father died, did you and Giovanni already know each other?'

The memory made her smile ever so faintly.

'Yes, we'd been together for three months. He took me into Papa's studio and—'

'OK, OK. When was your husband supposed to have embarked?'

'On the fourth of September.'

'Where?'

'At Gioia Tauro.'

'When did he leave here?'

'Very early the day before, on the third.'

'How?'

'By car.'

'Wait a minute. That means he was definitely in Gioia Tauro on the evening of the third. We need to find out what hotel he went to. And what he did.'

'But that's not what happened, Inspector. I left with him on the morning of the third. We took my car, in fact. We got there in the evening and went straight to his room.'

'His room?'

'Yes, for the last two years or so he's been renting a one-room flat with a bathroom and kitchenette.'

'Why?'

'Because very often Giovanni didn't have time to come and see me here. He would be in port for only two or three days . . . And so he would let me know so that when he came ashore I would be there waiting for him.'

'I see. And what did you do on the evening of the third?'

'We ate and then we—'

'Out? Did you eat out at a restaurant?'

157

'No, we ate at home. We'd bought a few things. And then we went to bed early. This time it was going to be a long journey.'

Better skip the nocturnal details. How was it possible that after years of marriage those two could think of nothing but engaging in that particular act? Maybe it was a Colombian thing.

'Did you receive any telephone calls?'

'There's no phone there. But nobody called on the mobile phone, either.'

'And the following morning?'

'Giovanni left at eight o'clock. I tidied up and left immediately afterwards. Which was a mistake.'

'Why?'

'Because I had no idea how tired I was. I had hardly slept a wink the night before and so, as I was driving, all at once I woke up as I was about to run into the sign for the state road for Lido di Palmi. Two men who were in the car behind me and who came to my aid said I had also run into the central reservation and made no sign of braking. They realized I was falling asleep.'

'Did you hurt yourself?'

'No, luckily. I went and rested at a motel nearby as my car was being repaired. They hoped to have it ready for me by the afternoon but didn't make it. So I spent the night at the motel and left the next day.'

'Have you been back to Gioia Tauro at any time since?'

She gave him a quizzical look.

'No. Why would I do that?'

'So the place should be in the condition you left it on the morning of September the fourth.'

'Of course.'

'Do you have the keys?'

'Of course.'

'And your husband his own set?'

'Yes.'

'Is there a cleaning woman who—'

'I always leave everything in order. And when I go back, I make sure that Giovanni finds the place all clean.'

'Give me the address.'

'Via Gerace 15, ground floor. You enter from the rear; there's a little gate.'

'Give Fazio the keys before he leaves.'

'Why?'

'Signora, we don't know how or why your husband disappeared. If he did it of his own free will, he very likely went back to that room after you left for Vigàta. And even if he disappeared at someone else's hands, it's possible that he was held in that room, against his will, by someone who knew him well.'

'I see.'

'Well, for the moment I think that's all.'

'Don't you want to choose a photo of Giovanni?'

'Ah yes, that's right.'

'Come with me into the bedroom. They're in there.'

At the sound of the word 'bedroom', Fazio, who the inspector had brought along as a watchdog, sprang to his feet.

'I'm coming too,' he said.

'No, you stay here,' said Montalbano.

Fazio sat down again, looking worried.

'Call me if you need me,' he muttered.

'Need you for what?' asked Dolores, genuinely puzzled.

'Well, in case there are too many photos, you know . . .' the inspector improvised.

In the bedroom the scent of cinnamon was so strong, it made him want to cough.

The bed was one of the biggest Montalbano had ever seen, a veritable drill-ground. You could have held manoeuvres, parades, and marches in it. At the foot of the bed there was a huge television and dozens of video-tapes. On top of the television was a video camera.

Montalbano was convinced that Dolores and her husband filmed themselves during certain exercises in the drill-ground, and then watched themselves afterwards so they could perfect them.

ELEVEN

Dolores, meanwhile, had opened the bottom drawer of the dresser and pulled out a packet of photographs that she spread out on the bed.

'These are the most recent, the ones we took at the home of that distant relative of Giovanni's. Take whichever ones you want.'

Montalbano picked up a few. In order to have a look at them herself, Dolores came up beside him, so close that her hip touched the inspector's.

They must have been taken at the end of a day in late August. The light was extraordinary. Two or three showed Dolores in a bikini. The inspector felt the point of contact between their two bodies heat up. When he moved slightly aside, she drew near again. Was she doing it on purpose, or did she really need to have physical contact with a man at all times?

'This is a really good one of Giovanni,' said Dolores, picking out a photo.

He was a good-looking man of about forty, tall and dark, with intelligent eyes, and an open, smiling face.

'All right, I'll take this one,' said the inspector. 'Don't forget to give Fazio the information on your husband: when he was born, where—'

'OK.'

'And whose beautiful house is this?' Montalbano asked, looking at a snapshot that showed Dolores, Giovanni, and some other people on a large terrace with a great many potted plants. He knew full well whose house it was, but he wanted to hear her say it.

'Oh, that's my husband's relative's house. His name is Don Balduccio Sinagra.'

Indeed there he was in the photo: Don Balduccio, sitting in a deckchair.

He was smiling. But Dolores had said his name with near indifference.

'Will that be enough?'

'Yes.'

'Would you help me put things away?'

'OK.'

She picked up the envelope and held it open for him, and he slipped in a first handful of photos. He had just inserted the second and last handful when she leaned slightly forward, grabbed his right hand, and planted her lips on its back. The inspector recoiled dramatically and was in danger of falling lengthwise onto the bed. Dolores, however, managed to keep her lips glued to his hand.

Montalbano, meanwhile, felt suddenly drained of all strength, all ability to resist. How many degrees had the temperature in the room risen?

Luckily Dolores raised her head and looked him straight in the eye. One could drown in that gaze.

'Help me,' she said. 'Without him, I'm ... Help me.'

Montalbano freed his hand, turned his back to her, and went into the living room, speaking perhaps too loudly.

'You, Fazio, take down her declaration, then have the lady give you the list of friends, the address in Gioia Tauro, and the keys.'

Fazio said nothing.

He was staring, spellbound, at the imprint of lipstick the woman's lips had left on the inspector's hand. The stigmata of St Salvo, who was certainly not a virgin but no less a martyr. Montalbano rubbed it with his other hand to make it disappear.

Dolores came in.

'I must be going now, signora. I think we'll have to meet again.'

'I'll show you out,' said Dolores.

'For heaven's sake, please don't bother!' said Montalbano, fleeing.

*

'Macannuco? Montalbano here.'

'Montalbano! Good to hear from you! How are you?'

'Not too bad. And yourself?'

'You remember that song we used to sing in class? *Whatever I say, whatever I do, / I always take it up the wazoo.* The situation hasn't changed.'

'Listen, Macannuco, I need you to do me a big favour.'

'For you, I'll do that and more.'

Macannuco headed the commissariat in the port of Gioia Tauro. Montalbano explained what he needed from him.

'Lemme get this straight, Montalbà. You're asking me to break down the door of an apartment in Via Gerace 15, photograph the place, and email you the photos?'

'Exactly.'

'Without a warrant?'

'Exactly.'

*

Fazio straggled back less than half an hour later.

'Jesus, what a dame!'

'Did you get everything we needed from her?'

'Yes, sir. There's only three names on the list of friends.'

'Listen, tell me in a little more detail the story of Balduccio and the Alfano guy he sent to Colombia.'

'Chief, did you notice how the lady kept talking about a "distant relative" without ever mentioning Balduccio Sinagra by name?'

'Actually, she did mention him by name. When we were in the bedroom looking through the photos. But she did it very offhandedly, as if she didn't know who Balduccio was. Do you think it's possible she doesn't know?'

'No. So, anyway, one day some twenty-odd years ago, Don Balduccio sends a second cousin, Filippo Alfano, to Colombia, to maintain direct contact with the big coke producers there. Filippo Alfano brings along his family, which consists of his wife and son, Giovanni, who at the time is fifteen. Then, sometime later, Filippo Alfano is shot and killed.'

'By the Colombians?'

'By someone from Colombia, definitely. But some people tell another version of this story. Some people, mind you.'

'I read you, go on.'

'They say it was Don Balduccio himself who had him killed.'

'And why?'

'I dunno, there were a lot of rumours. The most commonly accepted explanation is that Filippo Alfano took advantage of the situation, expanded his operations, and started thinking more about his own business than about Don Balduccio's, in the hope of taking his place.'

'And Balduccio prevented him. But he looked after the widow and son, according to what Dolores told us.'

'Which makes sense. It's in keeping with Don Balduccio's mentality.'

'So the son, Giovanni, has always kept his nose clean?'

'Chief, he's been in the sights of the narcotics authorities of at least two continents his whole life! With the line of work he's in? No, he's never tripped up, not even once.'

'Oh, listen, take this photo of Giovanni Alfano and have ten copies of it made for me. They may come in handy. Then have the three friends come in for questioning tomorrow morning, one hour apart. Oh, and one other thing. I want to know the exact date Balduccio Sinagra went into hospital.'

'Is it important?'

'Yes and no. I'm thinking of that anonymous letter that claimed Balduccio gave the order to have one of his couriers killed. If I'm not mistaken, Ballerini told Musante that Balduccio was hospitalized and in a coma in Palermo, and so Musante decided that Balduccio had nothing to do with it.'

'You're not mistaken.'

'Except that Dolores showed me a photo of Balduccio in which he looked just fine. I managed to get a glimpse of the date on the back: 28 August. Therefore Balduccio could have had all the time in the world to order a hit on whoever he liked before going into hospital. Make sense?'

'Makes sense.'

*

The inspector had just finished eating the way God had intended and was getting up from the table when Enzo approached.

'Inspector, where are you going to spend Christmas and New Year this year?'

'Why do you ask?'

'I wanted to let you know that if by any chance you're staying in Vigàta, the trattoria will be closed on the night of the thirty-first. But if you want to come to my place that night, I'd be honoured and pleased to have you.'

So now the tremendous pain in the arse of the holidays was about to begin! He couldn't stand them any more – not so much the holidays in themselves, but the annoying rituals of best wishes, presents, lunches, dinners, invitations and return invitations. And then the greeting cards expressing the hope that the coming year would be better than the one just ended – a vain hope, since every new year in the end turned out to be slightly worse than the one before.

Enzo's question had blocked his digestion like a blast of cold air. In vain he took his customary walk to the lighthouse at the end of the jetty. The effect was nil, his stomach still felt heavy.

As the final blow, he imagined the inevitable, imminent arguments with Livia – *Will you be coming to Boccadasse? No, you come to Vigàta* – on and on to the point of exhaustion or bickering.

*

'Ahh, Chief, Chief! Misser Giacchetta called! He says it wadn't so important 'n' so iss not so important f'you to call 'im cuz he's gonna call back.'

Fabio Giacchetti, the bank manager and new father. What might he have to say?

'When he calls back, put him through to me.'

'Ahh, Chief, I almos' forgot. Fazio called an' tol' me to tell yiz 'e knows when 'e's goin' inna haspitol.'

'Fazio's going into hospital?!' said Montalbano, alarmed.

'No, no, Chief, don' worry, I prolly din't say it right. So I'll try agin, so jus' bear wit' me a seccun. So, Fazio tol' me to tell yiz 'e knows when 'e – but he ain't Fazio, 'e's summon ellis – when 'e's gone inna haspitol.'

At last he understood: Fazio had learned the date of Balduccio Sinagra's admission to the clinic.

'And when was it?'

''E says it was the turd o' September.'

Confirmed. So Don Balduccio would have had time to give as many execution orders as he wanted. But why hadn't the people at Anti-Mafia reached the same conclusion?

Why had they taken the information given them by Narcotics as valid? Why were they so convinced the anonymous letter wasn't true? Or had they in fact investigated but didn't want anyone to know?

*

'Montalbano? This is Macannuco.'

'Hi. What's up? Did you do it?'

'Yes.'

'And?'

'First I have to ask you something.'

From his tone of voice, he seemed on edge. Maybe something had gone wrong. Or he'd had problems with a superior.

'Go on, ask your question.'

'Could you have a copy of a search warrant sent to me within an hour?'

'Within an hour? I can try.'

'Do it right away, I'm telling you.'

'Do you need to cover your back?'

'Yes. I can't not tell our prosecutor, who's quite the formalist, that I entered the Via Gerace apartment completely illegally.'

'Why do you have to tell him?!'

'Because.'

Maybe someone had seen them breaking down the door. It would have been amusing to watch if they'd been arrested by the carabinieri!

'Did you go there yourself?'

'Of course. Without a warrant, I had to be the one to take responsibility. Get me that warrant, and I'll let you know why I have to report everything to the prosecutor.'

'All right, but, in the meantime, did you take any photos? Could you send them to me?'

'There are four photos, and you'll be receiving them at any moment. Bye, talk to you soon.'

*

By the time Fazio returned, Montalbano had already spoken to Prosecutor Tommaseo, told him about Alfano's disappearance, obtained a warrant, and had it faxed from Montelusa to Macannuco.

Fazio looked befuddled.

'What's wrong?'

'What's wrong, Chief, is we were wrong.'

'Can you speak a little more clearly?'

'I compared the data on Giovanni Alfano that Dolores gave me with the missing-persons data. You remember when I said there wasn't anybody whose data matched up with the body we found in the *critaru*?'

'Yes, I remember.'

'Well, now there *is* somebody, and his information matches up with Alfano's. In every respect: age, height, probable weight.'

Now it was Montalbano's turn to look befuddled.

And as they were looking at each other, the door flew open with a crash that might have been a bomb. Montalbano and Fazio cursed in unison, while Catarella remained in the doorway, looking pensive.

'Well, aren't you going to come in?'

'Chief, I's thinkin' that maybe I oughta try knockin wit' my feet, since my 'and always slips.'

'No, instead you ought to try this: when you're in front of the door, instead of knocking, take out your gun and shoot once in the air. I'm sure it would make less noise. What is it?'

Catarella came in, went up to the desk, and set four photographs down on it.

'They's juss sint from Tauro Gioiosa an' I prinnit 'em.'

He left.

'You'd better be careful, Chief. The next time he comes in, the guy's gonna shoot just like you said,' said Fazio, worried. 'And it may start a revolution.'

'Don't worry about it,' said Montalbano. 'Come and have a look at these photos yourself.'

Fazio came up beside him.

The first one, which showed the bedroom, had been taken in such a way as to display the whole room. On the right was an open door through which one glimpsed the bathroom. The bed was almost as big as the one the Alfanos had in Vigàta, and there was an armoire, a chest of drawers, and two chairs. All in perfect order but for a pair of trousers tossed carelessly onto the bed.

The second shot showed a sort of living room with a kitchenette in the corner and hanging cupboards. There was also a small table with four chairs, two armchairs, a television, a sideboard, and a fridge. Next to the sink was an uncorked bottle of wine, a can of beer, and two glasses.

The third photo showed the bathroom. But the shot was taken so as to isolate the sink, toilet, and bidet. Here it was clear that whoever had last used the toilet had forgotten to flush, since the bowl was full of shit.

The fourth was an enlargement of the pair of trousers on the bed.

'Didn't the lady say she left the place in order?' said Fazio.

'Yeah. That means someone entered the apartment after she left.'

'The husband?'

'Maybe.'

'Definitely accompanied by someone else. There are two glasses.'

'Yeah.'

'What do you think, Chief?'

'At the moment I don't want to think about anything.'

'What are we going to do?'

'We have to show these photos to Dolores immediately. Call her right now and ask her if she can come here or if we should go there.'

*

Dolores Alfano showed them into the living room, after receiving them without so much as a smile. She was clearly nervous and mostly curious to know what the two men had to tell her. She didn't even ask if they wanted coffee or something to drink. Montalbano weighed his options. Should he get straight to the point or beat around the bush, given that she wasn't going to like what he had to tell her? Better not to waste any time.

'Signora,' he began, 'I believe I recall you saying this morning that it was your custom, when leaving the apartment in Gioia Tauro, to leave everything orderly and neat. Is that correct?'

'Yes.'

'And you don't have a cleaning woman?'

'I do the cleaning myself.'

'So, once you leave Gioia Tauro and lock up, nobody else goes inside. Is that correct?'

'That seems logical to me, no?'

'One more thing, signora. In your opinion, could your husband have lent the apartment to a friend who needed a place to stay, perhaps an associate passing through?'

'When he wasn't there, you mean?'

'Yes.'

'I would rule that out absolutely.'

'Why?'

'Because Giovanni is very possessive. Of me, of his things, of everything that belongs to him. You can imagine how he would feel about lending his apartment to someone...'

She stopped short when she saw Montalbano signal to Fazio, who handed him the envelope he was holding.

The inspector pulled out three photographs and laid them down on the table. The first was the photo of the bedroom, which Dolores recognized immediately.

'But that's ... May I?'

'Of course.'

Dolores picked it up, looked at it, and didn't say a word, but from her half-open mouth came a sort of faint, long lament. Then, photograph still in hand, she closed her eyes and leaned back in her chair. She remained that way for a moment, chest rising and falling with her anxious breath, waiting for the effect of what she'd seen to pass. Then she sighed deeply, opened her eyes, bent down brusquely, and grabbed the other two photos. She didn't even need to study them, and tossed them back onto the table.

She must have turned pale, because her skin, which was naturally dark, had now lightened to a kind of grey.

'Somebody ... somebody went in after I ... It's not possible ... I left everything in order ...'

Montalbano then took the fourth photograph out of the envelope, the enlargement of the shot of the trousers, and handed it to her.

'I know this is a difficult question, but can you tell me if these trousers belong to your husband?'

She took a long look at the photograph. Then she leaned back in her chair again, closed her eyes again. This time, however, a tear fell from her left eye. Only one, very round. It looked like a pearl. That single tear was more tragic, more desperate than a whole waterfall of tears. Dolores managed to say, in a soft voice:

'They're the ones he was wearing when he left to board the ship.'

'Are you sure?'

Without answering, Dolores Alfano stood up, went to a chest in the living room, opened a drawer, returned to the table with a magnifying glass in hand, and picked up the photo again. Then she passed the glass and photo to the inspector. She had regained complete control of herself.

'See? He left the belt in the trouser loops. If you look closely, the buckle is a large plate of copper with his initials interwoven, G and A. He had it made in Argentina.'

The inspector was unable to read the initials, but he could see that something had been carved into the copper plate.

'So it's clear your husband waited for you to leave before going back into the flat. And he came with some-one else.'

'But why?! To do what?!'

'Maybe he needed some time, was waiting for it to be a certain hour and didn't want to be seen out and about, since he had officially boarded his ship already. Does your husband drink wine?'

ANDREA CAMILLERI

'Yes, but he doesn't like beer.'

'Apparently whoever was with him did. Do you know if the beer and wine were already there in the apartment?'

'Yes. There was beer in the fridge, because I like to drink it.'

'As you can see, the bathroom was left a mess. Does your husband care about cleanliness and hygiene?'

'Inspector, anyone who spends long periods of time on a ship follows strict rules of hygiene. And my husband is a maniac for cleanliness.'

'So it couldn't have been him who left the bathroom in that condition.'

'Absolutely not. And he must not even have realized that the person with him hadn't—'

'Why would he have changed his trousers?'

'That's something I can't understand. Maybe he'd got them dirty or torn them.'

'It doesn't look like it in the photo.'

'I don't know what to say.'

'Did he have a change of clothes with him?'

'Of course. In two big bags he took away with him that morning.'

'Weren't there any clothes in the armoire?'

'No, he'd taken everything away with him.'

'So, once back in Via Gerace, your husband opened a bag, took out a pair of trousers and put them on instead of the ones he'd been wearing.'

'Apparently.'

TWELVE

Until that moment, Dolores Alfano had managed to stay calm and control herself. Now she began to tremble slightly. She still had a grey cast.

'Excuse me, I need to go to the bathroom,' she said, getting up.

She went out. She'd left the door open, and they could hear her vomiting.

'Fazio, have you got your phone with you?' asked the inspector, also getting up.

'Yes, sir.'

'Call Catarella and ask him for the number of the Gioia Tauro police, then call them and ask for Inspector Macannuco. Then pass the phone to me.'

'But where are you going now?'

'Out on the balcony to smoke a cigarette.'

He felt a weariness weighing down on him like a ton of iron. It had come over him all at once, with a thought that had flashed in his brain as he was studying the photo of the trousers. What a strange reaction!

Time was when he would have made an angry or sly remark. No longer. Only weariness and discouragement.

As he looked out the big window at the port – a steamship mooring, seagulls flying low, fishing boats laid up – a melancholy feeling, on top of his fatigue, welled up, bringing a lump into his gullet.

'I've got Macannuco on the line,' said Fazio, reaching over the windowsill and handing him the phone.

'Montalbano here. Did you get the warrant?'

'Yes, thanks.'

'I wanted to ask you if the trousers that were on the bed were dirty or torn.'

'Absolutely not.'

'Did you get any fingerprints?'

'No.'

'What do you mean, no?'

'My dear Salvo, somebody took great care to get rid of every last trace. A perfect job, professional. And you don't seem surprised. Did you expect as much?'

'Yes.'

'Let's see now if I can surprise you with some other news. In the bathroom ceiling, over the basin, there's a trapdoor.'

'It's not visible in the photo you sent.'

'That's because the shot's not taken from the right

angle. Anyway, I climbed a stepladder and opened it. There's a little sort of attic there, and I found an empty suitcase and a shoebox.'

'Which am I supposed to be surprised by, the suitcase or the shoebox?'

'The shoebox. It was also empty, but I noticed, on the bottom, a trace of some white powder, which I had tested.'

'Cocaine.'

'That's right. And that's why I had to inform the public prosecutor.'

'I understand. Thanks, Macannuco. I'll be in touch.'

He went back inside. Fazio was sitting in the armchair. Dolores still hadn't returned from the bathroom.

'What did Macannuco say?'

'I'll tell you later.'

Dolores came into the room. She had washed and changed her dress. But she hadn't recovered her vivacity. She looked withered, in her movements, her way of walking, and her eyes. She sat down with a sigh.

'I'm sorry, but I feel very tired.'

'We'll be leaving right away, signora,' said the inspector. 'But first I must ask you at least one question, which could be helpful to the investigation. Very helpful. I know it's painful for you to be asked at a time like this to remember the past, but I have no choice.'

'Go ahead.'

'How did you meet your husband?'

The question shocked Fazio, who looked at Montalbano with surprise. Signora Dolores winced before answering, as if from a shooting pain.

'He came to my father's office.'

'In Bogotá?'

'No, we were in Putumayo.'

Putumayo. The biggest drug-production centre in Colombia. Filippo Alfano had gone to the right place.

'The nurse had been absent for several days,' Dolores continued, 'and my father asked me to fill in for her.'

'Your father was a doctor?'

'A dentist.'

'And what sort of dental work did Giovanni need?'

She smiled at the memory.

'He'd fallen off his motorbike. Papa had to give him a bridge.'

What more did he need to know? Who's in grandma's bed? The big bad wolf. What's thirty minus two? Twenty-eight. He had known for at least the past half-hour who the dead man in the *critaru* was. But the fatigue was now making his legs ache. He got up from the armchair with some effort. Fazio also stood up.

'Thank you, signora. As soon as I have any news, I'll be sure to tell you.'

'Thank you,' said Dolores.

She didn't make a scene. Didn't scratch him, didn't twist his hand, didn't grab him by the lapels. The woman was dignified, composed, sober. Different. For the first time, the inspector felt a sense of genuine admiration for her.

*

'That woman's got balls!' Fazio said admiringly once they were on the street. 'I was expecting a hair-raising scene from her, and instead she controlled herself even better than a man.'

Montalbano didn't comment on this comment, but only asked: 'Were you aware that Pasquano, when he did the post-mortem on the *critaru* victim, found a bridge in the stomach?'

Fazio, who was bending down to unlock the car door, stopped halfway and looked up at him, stunned.

'He had a bridge in his stomach?'

'He most certainly did. Apparently, shortly before he was killed, the bridge came unstuck and he swallowed it. But it hadn't had time to pass through his body.'

Fazio was still bent down halfway.

'And there's more,' the inspector went on. 'The bridge was made, beyond the shadow of a doubt, by a dentist in South America. Now, you tell me. Who's in grandma's bed?'

'The big bad wolf,' Fazio replied automatically.

But immediately afterwards, he straightened himself abruptly, as the meaning of Montalbano's words finally penetrated his brain.

'So . . . according to you, the dead man in the *critaru*—'

'Is Giovanni Alfano. Not according to me, but according to Matthew,' Montalbano concluded. 'Anyway, you yourself said that Alfano's statistics corresponded pretty closely with those of the dead man.'

'Holy shit, you're right! But, I'm sorry, who's this Matthew?'

'I'll tell you later.'

'But why would anyone want to kill him?'

'You know what Macannuco told me? First, that all the fingerprints had been perfectly wiped away.'

'Professionals?'

'Apparently. The second thing he said is that they found an empty shoebox with traces of cocaine in it, in a sort of crawl space above the bathroom.'

'Holy shit!'

'Exactly. Which means that, despite the strict surveillance he was under, Alfano was mixed up with drugs. Maybe he was a courier.'

'That seems impossible.'

'Impossible or not, appearances lead us to conclude that those are the facts. So it's only natural to think that one fine day, following in his father's footsteps, Giovanni Alfano started behaving inappropriately in the eyes of his work provider.'

'Don Balduccio?'

'So it seems. And in Balduccio's eyes, that's a serious

offence. And intolerable. Giovanni, despite his father's treason, had always been treated like one of the family, to the point that not only did Balduccio not disown him, he actually helped him out when he was in Colombia. So Giovanni is a traitor to his own blood. He has to die. You with me so far?'

'Yes. Go on.'

'So Don Balduccio hatches an ingenious plan. He lets Giovanni leave for Gioia Tauro with Dolores, then has him kidnapped, brought back to Vigàta, killed, chopped up, and put in a rubbish bag. And he even tells his men to arrange things so that the body isn't discovered for some time. That way everyone will think that Giovanni boarded his ship. The plan is executed without a hitch, even though Balduccio in the meantime ends up in a clinic. Giovanni's wife, however, some two months after her husband sets sail, starts to get suspicious and comes and tells us about it.'

'But why all the drama of cutting him up into pieces and burying them at 'u critaru?'

'Have you ever read the Gospels, Fazio?'

'Never, Chief.'

'Bad.'

And he explained the whole story to him. When he had finished, Fazio was looking at him, open-mouthed.

'So it's as if Don Balduccio had left his signature!'

'Right. That's why it all makes sense, don't you think?'

'I certainly do. So what do we do now?'

'We take a little time.'

'And what about Signora Dolores?'

'For the moment there's no point in telling her anything more . . . It would only make her suffer and wouldn't help her at all. The body's in such bad shape she wouldn't even be able to identify it.'

'Chief, I was just thinking that whoever wrote the anonymous letter to the Anti-Mafia office knew everything.'

'Yeah. When the time is right we'll rub Musante's nose in it, for having dismissed that letter too quickly. But before we make any moves, give me a day to think things over.'

'Whatever you say, Chief. What are you doing now, coming to the office?'

'Yes, I want to pick up my car and go home.'

*

Fazio parked, and they got out.

'Chief, could I come into your office for a few minutes? I'd like to talk to you about something,' said Fazio, who hadn't opened his mouth the whole way back to the station.

'Of course.'

'Ahh, Chief, Chief!' said Catarella, racing out of his cupboard, 'I gots a litter f'yiz I's asposta give yiz poissonally in poisson.'

Looking around himself with a conspiratorial air, he pulled an envelope out of his pocket and handed it to the inspector.

'Who gave it to you?'

'Isspector Augello did. An' he said I's asposta put it in yer hand the minnit I sawr yiz.'

'And where is he?'

''E stepped out momentaneously, Chief, but 'e says 'e'll be back.'

Montalbano pushed on towards his office, with Fazio following.

'Have a seat, Fazio, while I see what Mimì wants.'

The envelope was open. There were only a few lines.

Dear Salvo,

This is to remind you that you promised to let me know as soon as possible whether or not you plan to assign me the only important case on our hands at the moment.

Mimì

He handed the note to Fazio, who read it and gave it back without saying a word.

'What do you make of it?'

'Chief, I already told you I don't think it's a good idea to assign a case like this to Inspector Augello. But you're the one who gives the orders around here.'

Montalbano put the note and envelope in his jacket pocket.

'What did you want to tell me?'

'Chief, would you please explain to me what it is you need to think over?'

'I don't understand.'

'You said you needed a day to think things over with regard to Giovanni Alfano.'

'So?'

'What's to think over? It all seems so clear to me!'

'You mean it seems clear to you that Giovanni Alfano was killed on orders from Balduccio?'

'*Matre santa*, Chief, you said it yourself!'

'I said that the facts that we have come to know lead us inevitably to this conclusion.'

'Why, could there be any other conclusion?'

'Why not?'

'But what are your doubts based on?'

'I'll give you an example, OK? Don't you think there's a certain inconsistency in Balduccio's way of going about things?'

'And what would that be?'

'Can you explain to me why Balduccio would blithely let Giovanni Alfano leave for Gioia Tauro? The only possible answer is that he didn't want him killed here in Vigàta, where he would have almost immediately been implicated in our investigation, but far from his territory. And that's probably what happened.'

'So where's the inconsistency?'

'The inconsistency is in bringing the body back here – that is, back into his own territory.'

'But he couldn't have done otherwise, Chief!'

'Why not?'

'Because he had to set an example, so that other potential traitors in the family would think twice about betraying him!'

'Right. But then he might as well have him killed here and be done with it!'

Fazio remained a little doubtful.

'And there's more,' Montalbano continued. 'You want to hear it?'

'Sure.'

'Let's imagine that Balduccio sends a real professional to Gioia Tauro, someone who knows his trade and never makes mistakes.'

'And in fact he left no fingerprints whatsoever,' said Fazio.

'Yeah. But he left a little cocaine inside a shoebox in the crawl space. Does that seem to you like an insignificant fuck-up? For us, the cocaine means a direct connection to Balduccio. So, in short, this so-called professional fails to do the very thing he's supposed to do, remove every notion that any cocaine has ever passed through the place. Doesn't that seem strange to you?'

'So it does . . .'

'And shall I throw down my ace while we're at it?'

'Might as well . . .' said Fazio, resigned.

'Why leave a pair of trousers in plain view on the bed? It's clear they belong to Giovanni Alfano – you can even see the initials on the belt buckle. Not only that, but there was no reason for Alfano to change his trousers. All they had to do was put those trousers back in their place in the armoire, and we never would have known that Alfano went back to Via Gerace. So what, then, is the purpose of those trousers? Is it to let us know that Alfano, by force or by his own choice, returned to his apartment? And who benefits from such information? If it was a mistake, it was a huge one, because Signora Dolores noticed immediately that the apartment was not the way she left it. There was even shit in the toilet bowl! Can you tell me what need there was for the professional to return to the apartment with Giovanni? Wouldn't it have been better to get rid of him while he was on his way to board the ship? The only possible explanation is that he went back to the apartment to eliminate any trace of a possible connection with Balduccio. But that's exactly what he didn't do! So, then, why go back there with Alfano? There's something here that doesn't make sense to me.'

'Enough. I surrender,' said Fazio, who got up and left.

*

'Chief? 'At'd be a Mr Lambrusco.'

'What's he want?'

''E says you summonsed 'im fer tomorrow mornin'.'

'So, let him come tomorrow morning.'

''E don't got the possibility, Chief. Says how tomorrow mornin' 'e can't 'cuz tomorrow mornin' he gotta go to Milan emergently tomorrow mornin'.'

'All right then, put him on.'

'I can't put 'im on in so much as 'at this Lambrusco's 'ere poissonally in poisson.'

'Then send him in.'

He was a fortyish man with beard, moustache and spectacles, tiny in stature and all polished and shiny, from his hair to his shoes.

'Hello, I'm Carlo Dambrusco. I'm sorry, I know you summoned me for tomorrow morning, but since tomorrow I have to—'

'What was this in reference to?'

'Well, I . . . I believe I gathered that . . . well, in short, I'm a friend of Giovanni Alfano.'

'Ah, yes. Please sit down.'

'Has something happened to Giovanni?'

'He was supposed to board a ship and never turned up.'

'He didn't turn up?'

'No. His wife has filed a report.'

Dambrusco seemed genuinely stunned by the news.

'He didn't board the ship?' he asked again.

'No.'

'So where did he go?'

'That's what we're trying to find out.'

'The last time I saw him . . .'

'When was that?'

'Let me think . . . The first of September.'

'Go on.'

'He said goodbye to me because he was going to set sail two or three days later . . . He made no indication to me that he didn't intend to . . . He takes his work very seriously.'

'Does he confide in you much?'

'Good heavens . . . We were very good friends in childhood, before he left for Colombia . . . Then we got back in touch, later on, but it was different. We were friends, but we weren't so close that . . .'

'I see. But did he confide in you?'

'In what sense?'

'In the way that a friend confides in a friend. For example, did he ever talk to you about his relations with his wife? Did he ever mention whether, on his travels, he met any other women . . . ?'

Dambrusco shook his head emphatically and repeatedly.

'I really don't think so. He's a serious person, not the kind to take love affairs lightly. In any case, he is very much in love with Dolores. He has in fact confided to me that he misses her very much when he's at sea.'

'And what about Dolores?'

'I don't understand.'

'Does Dolores miss her husband very much when he is at sea?'

Carlo Dambrusco thought about this a moment.

'I honestly can't say. Every time I've met Dolores she's been with Giovanni. I've never had a chance to talk to her when he wasn't there.'

'Fine, but that really wasn't what I meant.'

'I realize that. But, to answer your question, no, I've never heard any malicious gossip about Dolores's behaviour.'

'One last question. As far as we know, Giovanni, when at home in Vigàta, had only three friends with whom he socialized, you being one of them. I'll be talking to the other two tomorrow morning. Which of the three was he closest to?'

Dambrusco did not hesitate.

'Michele Tripodi. Who's waiting outside.'

'You mean he's here?'

'Yes. He brought me here in his car. I have to take mine to Milan tomorrow, and it's still at the mechanic's.'

'Would you do me a favour? Could you ask him if he would come in to see me now instead of tomorrow morning? It shouldn't take but five minutes.'

'Of course.'

THIRTEEN

Michele Tripodi also looked to be about forty but, unlike Dambrusco, who was diminutive and skinny, he was tall, athletic, and genial, a handsome specimen.

'Carlo told me Giovanni has disappeared. Is it true? Does Dolores know?'

'It was Mrs Alfano herself who got things moving.'

'But when would he have disappeared? Dolores, when she got back from Gioia Tauro, told me Giovanni had boarded his ship.'

'That's what Giovanni led her to believe, or was forced to have her believe.'

Michele Tripodi's face darkened.

'I don't like that.'

'You don't like what?'

'What you just said. Giovanni never deceives Dolores, nor would he have any reason to make her believe something that wasn't true.'

'Are you sure?'

'About what?'

'About both things.'

'Listen, Inspector. Giovanni is so taken by Dolores, I mean physically taken, that he's not sure, he told me, that he could even make love to another woman.'

'Does he have any enemies?'

'I don't know whether during the long sea voyages ... at any rate, I think he would have mentioned it to me.'

'Listen, this is a delicate subject, but I have to ask you about it. If Giovanni has been kidnapped, couldn't this be a sort of vendetta by proxy?'

Michele Tripodi understood at once.

'You mean a vendetta against the Sinagras?'

'Yes.'

'You see, Inspector, Giovanni felt very indebted, and grateful, to Don Balduccio, who helped him out when his father died ... But Giovanni's an honest man; he has no truck with the Sinagras' business ... And he always felt ashamed of what his father, Filippo, did in Colombia ... It's true, of course, that whenever he comes to Vigàta he pays a call on Don Balduccio, no doubt about it, but it's not as if they're so close that—'

'I understand. As far as you know, has Giovanni ever used cocaine?'

Michele Tripodi started laughing. A hearty, full-bellied laugh.

'Are you kidding? Giovanni hates drugs of any kind!

He doesn't even smoke! And he even made Dolores give it up! Remember how his father was killed? Well, that fact marked him for life, and he has behaved accordingly.'

'I'm sorry, but I have another delicate question to ask you. It's about Dolores. It seems there are two conflicting opinions about her in town.'

'Inspector, Dolores is a beautiful woman who is forced to remain alone too often and for too long. And perhaps she's a bit too impulsive, and a bit too expansive, and this can sometimes give rise to misunderstandings.'

'Tell me one.'

'One what?'

'Give me an example of one such misunderstanding.'

'Well, I don't know . . . After she'd been in Vigàta for about a year a boy, an eighteen-year-old from a good family, started serenading her, literally singing serenades to her, and then started harassing her on the phone, and one time even tried to enter her apartment . . . Dolores had to call the carabinieri . . .'

'Only eighteen-year-olds? No adults?'

'Well, about two years ago there was a more serious episode where a butcher lost his head over her . . . doing ridiculous things like sending her a bouquet of roses every day . . . Eventually he had to move to Catania, and poor Dolores's persecutions ended there, fortunately.'

Montalbano laughed.

'Yes, I'd heard that story of the love-smitten butcher before . . . His name was Pecorella, if I'm not mistaken . . .'

'No, Pecorini,' Tripodi corrected him.

*

Was it important to know that the butcher who rented his house to Mimì for his amorous trysts had fallen in love with Dolores Alfano two years before? At first glance, it appeared not. But there was another question that had come into the inspector's head the moment Tripodi had told him the story of the butcher. Tripodi said that to rid herself of the boy who was bothering her, Dolores had called the carabinieri. But he didn't say what action Dolores had taken in the butcher's case. She certainly hadn't asked the carabinieri for help on that occasion. The butcher, however, had resolved the problem by moving to Catania. And this was where the question arose: why, from one day to the next, had he moved away from Vigàta if he was so in love with Dolores? What could have happened to him?

'Fazio! Into my office, quick! Fazio!'

'What is it, Chief?'

'You remember Pecorini?'

'The butcher? Yes.'

'I want to know, by tomorrow morning at the latest, why he left Vigàta two years ago and opened a butcher's shop in Catania.'

'All right, Chief. But what did this Pecorini do, sell meat with mad-cow disease or something?'

*

It was now late, and the inspector felt mighty hungry. Just as he was standing up, the telephone decided to ring. He hesitated a moment, wondering whether or not he should answer, but a goddamned motherfucking sense of duty got the better of him.

'Chief! Ahh, Chief! That'd be Mr Giacchetta.'

The inspector remembered that Giacchetti had asked for him.

'Show him in.'

'I can't, Chief, seeing as how he's in telephonic communication.'

'Then put him through.'

'Inspector Montalbano? This is Fabio Giacchetti, the bank manager who ... Do you remember me?'

'Of course I remember you. How are your wife and child?'

'Very well, thanks.'

And he stopped talking.

'So?' the inspector prodded him.

'Well, now that I'm on the phone and talking to you, I'm not sure if I really ought to ...'

Jesus, what a pain! The inspector remembered that the bank manager was one of those people who were always taking one step forward, two steps back, a ditherer born and bred, an expert in the art of shilly-shallying. He didn't feel like wasting any more time.

'Let me be the judge of whether you ought to or not. What did you want to tell me?'

'But it may be something of no importance...'

'Listen, Mr Giacchetta—'

'Giacchetti. All right, I'll tell you, even though it's not ... Well, I saw the car again, I'm sure of it.'

'What car?'

'The one that tried to run the woman over ... Remember?'

'Yes. You've seen it again?'

'Yes, yesterday. It was right in front of me at a red light. This time I took down the licence number.'

'Now, are you quite sure that it was the same car, Mr Giacchetti?'

A careless question, in which Giacchetti got lost and drowned.

'*Quite* sure, you ask? How could I possibly be one hundred per cent sure? Sometimes I'm sure, and other times no. At certain moments I could swear to it, and at others I feel I really can't. How could I...?'

'Let's pretend this is one of the moments when you feel absolutely certain.'

'Well, all right ... On top of everything else, I have to tell you that the car from the other night had a broken left rear light, and this one did, too.'

'You should know, Mr Giacchetti, that nothing

else has come of the episode you witnessed the other night.'

'Oh, really?' Giacchetti asked, disappointed.

'Yes. So, if you want, you can go ahead and give me the licence-plate number, but I don't think it will serve any purpose.'

'So, what should I do? Give you the number or not?'

'Please do.'

'BG 329 ZY,' Mr Giacchetti said rather listlessly.

'A kiss for the baby.'

*

Had everyone finally finished aggravating him? Could he now go home and think quietly about everything he had just learned, sitting on the veranda as the splashing surf slowly untied the knot of thoughts in his brain?

He closed the door to his office.

'I'll be seeing you, Cat.'

''Ave a g'night, Chief.'

He went outside and headed to his car. Mimì Augello must have come back to the office, since his car was parked so close to the inspector's that Montalbano had to turn sideways to squeeze between them. He got in the car, turned on the ignition, and drove off. Having gone barely ten yards down the street, he slammed on the brakes, eliciting a riot of curses and horn-blasts behind him.

He had seen something. And half of his brain wanted

to bring what he had seen into focus, while the other half refused, not wanting to believe the information his eyes had transmitted to it.

'Get out of the way, arsehole!' yelled an angry motorist, passing close by.

Montalbano threw the car into reverse though he couldn't see a thing, a sudden deluge of sweat pouring down from his brow and forcing him to keep his eyes half shut. At last he was back in the police station car park. He stopped, ran his arm over his face to wipe away the sweat, opened the car window, and looked. And there was the broken rear light, there the licence plate BG 329 ZY.

The car belonged to Mimì Augello.

A violent cramp like the stab of a knife seized his entrails and twisted them, triggering a gush of acidic, sickly sweet liquid that rose up into his throat. He got out of the car in a hurry and, leaning on the boot, started vomiting, throwing up his very soul.

*

Back home in Marinella, he realized that not only had his appetite completely vanished, but he also no longer felt like thinking. He opened the French windows to the veranda. The evening was too cold for a swim. He grabbed a bottle of whisky and two glasses, unplugged the telephone, went into the bathroom, took off his clothes, filled the bath, and got in.

It was a good remedy. Two hours later, he had nearly

emptied the bottle, the water had turned cold, but he had closed his eyes and was sleeping.

He woke up around four in the morning, freezing to death in the bath. So he had a scalding-hot shower and drank a big mugful of espresso.

Now he was ready to do some thinking, even though he could still feel a bit of nausea lurking at the back of his throat. He took a sheet of paper and a pen, sat down at the dining table, and started writing a letter to himself to put his thoughts in order.

Dear Salvo,

While you were vomiting in the car park, two words were hammering away at your brain: cahoots *and* conspiracy.

Two words you let float around inside you, not wanting to clarify their relationship to each other. Because, if you did, you wouldn't at all like what you saw. Namely, that Mimì Augello and Dolores Alfano are in cahoots, and conspiring to do something.

Let me try to clarify. There is no doubt that Mimì and Dolores are lovers and that they meet at the house of Pecorini the butcher. Taking a rough guess, their relationship must have begun in September, a few days after Giovanni Alfano was supposed to have boarded his ship.

Who initiated the love affair? Mimì? Or was it Dolores? This is an important point, even if it doesn't make much substantive difference. I'll try to explain a little better by backtracking.

From the moment the stranger's body was found at 'u critaru, Mimì started insisting that I assign the investigation to him.

Why that particular investigation? The answer might be: because it's the only important case we have on our hands at the moment.

This explanation holds up until I discover, with near certainty, that the critaru corpse has a first and last name: Giovanni Alfano. Who happens to be Dolores's missing husband. This changes things radically, and raises some unfortunately inevitable questions, which I shall now submit to you, spacing them sufficiently apart so that each has its proper relief.

— Did Mimì know that sooner or later I would identify the body as belonging to his mistress's husband?

— If so, how did Mimì know the body was Giovanni Alfano's before we connected the critaru corpse with Dolores?

— Is Mimì being pressured or sexually blackmailed by Dolores to have the investigation assigned to him?

— Is it possible Mimì is pressuring me against his own will, because he can't or doesn't know how to say no to Dolores?

— Have the two been having terrible quarrels because of this? It would appear they have, based on the scene that Fabio Giacchetti witnessed.

— Who could have told Mimì that the corpse in the critaru was his mistress's husband? It could only have been Dolores.

— *Did Dolores therefore know that her husband not only didn't board his ship, but had been murdered?*

— *Why, after the body was discovered, did Dolores come to the police station? There can only be one answer: because she wants to lead me, through skilful, intelligent manipulation, to the conclusion that the murder victim is her husband.*

— *She also wants to lead me to another inevitable conclusion: that the person who murdered Giovanni is Balduccio Sinagra.*

— *Two questions, therefore, arise here. Did Dolores latch on to Mimì because he was my second-in-command and she thus hoped to control the course of the investigation through him? Or did Dolores only discover afterwards that Mimì was my second-in-command and then decide to take advantage of the situation? In either case, Dolores's purpose remains the same.*

— *Are Mimì and Dolores therefore plotting together to force me to turn the case over to Mimì?*

— *Does Mimì want it publicly known that he has insistently asked me to assign him the case so as to avoid conflict with Dolores?*

— *And if this is how things stand, how would you define Mimì's behaviour towards you?*

At this point he had to stop, as his nausea had suddenly returned, stirring up a nasty, bitter sort of spittle in his mouth. He got up and went out onto the veranda. It was still dark outside. Not wanting to remain standing, he sat down on the bench.

How to describe Mimì's behaviour?

He knew the answer. It had come to him at once, but he hadn't wanted to say it or write it down.

Mimì had been disloyal to him; there could no longer be any doubt about this.

It wasn't because he had a lover. That sort of thing, and Mimì's private life in general, were of no concern to him. Even this time it would have been of no concern to him – though Mimì was married with a young son – had Livia not dragged him into it.

No, the disloyalty had begun the moment Mimì realized that Dolores wanted something from him not as a lover but as a police officer. Although his vanity as a lady-killer must have taken quite a blow, he hadn't been able or willing to break up with Dolores. Maybe he was too taken with her. Dolores was, after all, the kind of woman who could reduce a man to the state of a postage stamp stuck to her skin. So, at that point, Mimì should have come to him and said, with an open heart: 'Look, Salvo, I got involved in this affair, but then this and this happened, and now I need your help to get me out of these straits.' They were friends, weren't they? But there was more.

Not only had Mimì told him nothing about the predicament he was in; but, faced with a choice between him and Dolores, he had chosen Dolores. He had teamed up with her to force him, Montalbano, to take certain steps. Mimì had thus acted in the woman's interest. And a friend who acts not in your interest but in the interest of another without telling you, what has he done, if not betrayed your friendship?

At last the inspector was able to say it. Mimì was a traitor.

That word, *traitor*, once it had formed in his mind, blocked his thought process. For a brief moment the inspector's brain was a total void. And the void became silence – not only an absence of words, but of even the slightest sound. The bright line barely visible in the darkness, formed by the surf at the edge of the beach, moved ever so gently back and forth, as always, except that now it no longer made its usual breathlike hiss. Now there was nothing. And the throbbing of the diesel engine of a fishing boat whose lights shone wanly in the distance should have been audible from the veranda. But there was nothing. It was as though someone had turned off the soundtrack.

Then, within that silence of the world, perhaps of the universe, Montalbano heard a brief sound arise, unpleasant and strange, followed by another just the same, and still another, also the same. What was it?

It took him a while to realize that the sound was coming from him. He was crying inconsolably.

✢

He made an effort to squash the desire to let the whole thing slide all the way to hell and bail out in any way he could. Because that's the way he was. He was a man capable of understanding many things that others couldn't or wouldn't; moments of weakness, failures of courage, insolent disregard, lapses of attention, lies, ugly acts with ugly motives, things done out of laziness, boredom, self-interest, and so on. But he could never understand or forgive bad faith and betrayal.

'Oh, yeah? My valiant knight, peerless and fearless, says he can never forgive betrayal?'

'Yes, it's something I can't even conceive of. And you, who are me, know this well.'

'So how is it, then, that you've forgiven yourself?'

'Me? There's nothing I have to forgive myself for!'

'Are you really so sure? Would you please be so kind as to backtrack a few evenings in your memory?'

'Why, what happened?'

'Have you forgotten? Have we repressed this little fact? What happened is that you felt every bit as dejected as you do tonight, and for the same reason, except that then you had Ingrid beside you. Who comforted you. And, boy, did she ever comfort you.'

'Well, that happened because—'

'Montalbà, the whys and wherefores for such an act are all well and good, but the act remains the same: it's called betrayal.'

'You know what I say? I say that all this is happening because of that damn critaru, because of the potter's field.'

'Explain what you mean.'

'*I think that place, which is the place of the ultimate betrayal, where the betrayer betrays his own life, is cursed. Whoever passes near it, in one way or another, becomes contaminated with betrayal. I betrayed Livia, Dolores betrays Mimì, Mimì betrays me...*'

'*All right, then, if that's the way it is, then get Mimì the hell out of there. You are all — indeed we are all — in the same boat.*'

He got up, went inside, sat down, and resumed writing to himself.

FOURTEEN

And so, dear Salvo, as you see, such is the fine result I get by putting those two words together. But, if that's the way it is, quite a few other questions remain. Question number one: how did Dolores find out that Giovanni had been kidnapped and murdered by someone sent by Balduccio? Number two (with follow-up): why is Dolores so certain that it was Balduccio who had Giovanni killed? What kind of relationship did Giovanni and Balduccio have?

Number three: why does Dolores want to control the investigation through Mimì?

Possible answer to question number one:

Dolores told us she fell asleep at the wheel on the way back from Gioia Tauro and didn't get back to Vigàta until the next day, after spending the night in a motel. It's possible, on the other hand, that what she said is not true. That is, that she remained in Gioia Tauro for reasons of her own, and thus found out that Giovanni had not been able to board his ship because he'd been kidnapped by Balduccio's men. But why, then, not tell us this? Perhaps because it would only be a conjecture on her part, if she had no proof. Or perhaps because

she didn't know how her husband was killed and where the body was.
She only learned this when Mimì told her about the dismembered
corpse at 'u critaru.

Possible answer to question two:

Here there can be only one answer. Giovanni was a courier for
Balduccio. He must have been very good at it. And Dolores must
have been well aware of this activity. One day, however, he 'betrays'
Balduccio, who then has him killed. Dolores therefore hasn't the
slightest doubt about who ordered her husband's elimination.

Possible answer to question three:

Dolores knows — because Giovanni has surely told her — how
intelligent and shrewd old Balduccio is. She is moved by an irresistible
desire for revenge. She wants Balduccio to pay, and she knows that
the old Mafioso is capable of beating the justice system, as he has done
so many times in the past. With Mimì under her control, she hopes to
avert this danger, since she will never let him give up the fight against
Balduccio.

Dear Salvo, I have bored myself to tears writing to you. I've
said the essential. Now it's up to you.

Good luck.

*

Day was dawning. As he stood up from the table, cold
shivers ran up and down his spine. He undressed and got
into a bath so hot it filled the room with steam. When
he came out he was red as a lobster. He shaved, made a
pot of coffee, and drank his customary mugful. Then he
went into the bedroom, got dressed, took out an over-

night bag, put in a shirt, a pair of pants, a pair of socks, two handkerchiefs, and a book he was reading. Going back into the dining room, he re-read the letter he'd written to himself, brought it out to the veranda, and set fire to it with his lighter. He glanced at his watch. Almost 6:30. He went inside and dialled a number on the land line, slipping his mobile phone into his pocket.

'Hello?' answered Fazio.

'Montalbano here. Did I wake you up?'

'No, Chief. What is it?'

'Listen, I have to leave.'

Fazio became alarmed.

'Are you going to Boccadasse? What happened?'

'I'm not going to Boccadasse. I hope to be back this evening, or tomorrow morning at the latest. If I get back tonight I'll give you a ring, even if it's late. All right?'

'Yes, sir.'

'Don't forget that thing I asked you about. You absolutely must find out why Pecorini left Vigàta two years ago.'

'Don't worry.'

'This morning one of Alfano's friends is coming to the station. I talked to two others yesterday evening. I want you to question the one today.'

'All right.'

'The keys Dolores gave you to the apartment in Gioia Tauro, where are they?'

'On my desk, in an envelope.'

'I'm going to take them. Oh, and listen. If you happen to run into Inspector Augello today, don't tell him I've gone to Gioia Tauro.'

'Chief, he doesn't talk to any of us any more. But if he happens to ask me, what do I tell him?'

'Tell him I've gone to the hospital for a routine check-up.'

'You, go to the hospital of your own free will? He'll never believe it! Can't you think of anything better?'

'You think of something. But he mustn't suspect in any way that I'm doing something related to the *critaru* murder.'

'I'm sorry, Chief, but even if he does suspect something, what's the problem?'

'Just do as I say and don't argue.'

The inspector hung up.

Ah, how foul and swampy, how treacherous the ground around the potter's field!

*

Could he have spared himself the journey he was about to make? A journey which, for as poor a driver as him, represented a major effort? Of course, with the help of a good road map, he needn't even have left home. But going in person to see how things stood wasn't only the better, more serious course of action; it was also possible that the place itself, when seen with his own eyes, would suggest some other, new hypothesis for him to consider. But despite all the justifications he kept coming up with for making this trip, he knew he hadn't yet admitted the real reason for it. Once past Enna, however, when, on the left, he began to glimpse the mountains in whose folds lay towns like Assoro, Agira, Regalbuto, and Centuripe, he understood why he had left Marinella. Without a doubt, the investigation did have something to do with it. But the truth was that he wanted to see the landscape of his youth again, the one he had all around him when he was a deputy inspector at Mascalippa. Wait a second! Hadn't he found that same landscape depressing at the time? Didn't the very air in Mascalippa get on his nerves, because it smelled of straw and grass? All true, all sacrosanct. A line of Brecht came to mind: 'Why should I love the windowsill from which I fell as a child?' But that line still didn't quite say it, he thought. Because sometimes, when you're already almost old, the hated windowsill from which you fell as a little kid comes urgently back into your memory, and you would even go on a pilgrimage to see it again, if you could see it the way you did then, with the eyes of innocence.

Is this what you've come looking for? he asked himself as he rolled along the Enna to Catania autostrada at a snail's pace, driving to distraction all the other motorists unfortunate enough to be travelling the same route. *Do you think that seeing those mountains from afar, breathing that air from afar,*

*will bring back the ingenuousness, the naivety, the enthusiasm of your
first years with the police? Come on, Inspector, get serious, accept that
what you've lost is gone for ever.*

He suddenly accelerated, leaving the landscape behind.
The Catania–Messina autostrada wasn't too busy, and he
was able to board the twelve-thirty ferry across the straits.
Thus, since he had left home at seven, it had taken him
five and a half hours to go from Vigàta to Messina. It
would have taken somebody like Fazio, driving as he nor-
mally did, two hours less.

As soon as the ferry had passed the statue of the
Blessed Virgin, which wishes happiness and good health
to all voyagers, and begun to dance on the mildly choppy
sea, the salty air stirred up a beastly hunger in Montalbano's stomach. The night before, he hadn't had a chance
to eat anything. He quickly climbed a small staircase that
led to the bar. On the counter was a small mountain of
piping-hot *arancini*. He bought two and went out on deck
to eat them. Attacking the first, he reduced it by half
with a single bite, and of this half, he swallowed a good
portion. He realized his grave mistake at once. How
could they call *arancini* these rice balls fried in hundred-
year-old oil and cooked by a chef suffering from violent
hallucinations? And how acidic the meat sauce was!
He spat the rest of the *arancino* he had in his mouth into
the sea, and the remaining whole and half *arancini* met the
same watery end. He went back to the bar and drank a
beer to get rid of the nasty taste. Later, as he was easing

his car out of the ferry, that little bit of foul *arancino*, combined with the beer, bubbled up into his throat. The acid burned so badly that, without realizing it, he swerved and suddenly found himself sideways on the ramp, with the car's nose pointing out over the water.

'What the hell are you doing? What the hell are you doing?' yelled the sailor who was directing the disembarkation.

Sweating all over, the inspector coaxed the car, an inch at a time, back into the proper position, while the eyes of the man driving the HGV behind him seemed to say he was ready to slam him from behind and send him the fuck onto the dock or into the sea, take your pick.

At Villa San Giovanni he went and ate at a hauliers' restaurant where he'd already been twice before. And this third time he was not disappointed either. After an hour and a half at the table, that is, around three o'clock in the afternoon, he got back in his car and headed towards Gioia Tauro. He took the autostrada, and in a flash he was already past Bagnara. Continuing on the A3, he was about twelve miles from Gioia Tauro when he decided to take the final stretch nice and slow, looking for the state road to Lido di Palmi. There was a state road for Palmi, but not for Lido di Palmi. How could that be? He was sure he hadn't missed it and driven past. He decided to continue to Gioia Tauro. Leaving the autostrada, he headed towards town and stopped at the first petrol station he found.

'Listen, I need to go to Lido di Palmi. Should I take the autostrada?'

'The autostrada doesn't go there — or, rather, you would have to follow a long and complicated route. You're better off taking the state road, which'll take you down the shoreline. It's a lot nicer.'

The man explained how to get to the state road.

'One more thing, I'm sorry. Could you tell me where Via Gerace is?'

'You'll pass it on the way to the state road.'

*

Via Gerace 15 consisted of a little apartment that must have originally been a rather large garage. It was the first of four identical apartments situated one beside the other, each with a little gate and a tiny garden. Beside the door was a rubbish bin. The four flats were situated behind a rather tall building of some ten storeys. No doubt they were used as crash pads or pieds-à-terre for people passing through. The inspector got out of the car, took from his pocket the keys he had taken from Fazio's desk, opened the little gate, closed it behind him, opened the door, and closed this too. Macannuco had done a good job entering the place without forcing the locks. The apartment was quite dark, and Montalbano turned on the light.

There was a tiny entrance hall that hadn't been photographed; it had barely enough room for a coat-rack and a small, low piece of furniture with one drawer and a small lamp on top, which illuminated the space. The kitchen looked the same as in the photograph, but now the cupboards were open, as was the fridge; and bottles, boxes, and packages had been scattered higgledy-piggledy across the table.

The search team had passed through the bedroom like a tornado. Alfano's trousers were balled up on the floor. In the bathroom, they had dismantled the flushing system and exposed all the pipes, breaking the wall. The trapdoor directly above the basin was left open, and there was a folding stepladder beside the bidet. Montalbano moved it under the trapdoor and climbed it. The storage space was empty. Apparently the forensics team had taken the suitcase and shoebox away with them.

He climbed down, went back into the entrance hall, and opened the drawer on the little stand. Stubs of electricity and gas bills. Sticking out from under the stand, whose legs were barely an inch and a half tall, was the white corner of an envelope. Montalbano bent down to pick it up. It was an unopened bill from Enel, the electricity company. He opened it. The payment deadline on it was 30 August. It hadn't been paid. He put it back under the stand and was about to turn off the light when he noticed something.

He went up to the little stand again, ran a finger over it, picked up the lamp, put it back down, opened the door, went out, closed it behind him, and lifted the lid of the rubbish bin. It was empty. There were only a few stains of rust at the bottom. He put it back in its place, opened the little gate, was about to close it again behind him, when a voice above him called out:

'Who are you, may I ask?'

It was a fiftyish woman who must have weighed twenty stones or more, with the shortest legs Montalbano had ever seen on a human being. A giant ball. She was looking out from a balcony on the first floor of the tall building, directly above the Alfanos' apartment.

'Police. And who are you?'

'I'm the concierge.'

'I'd like to talk to you.'

'So talk.'

A half-open window on the second floor of her building then opened all the way, and a girl who looked about twenty came forward, resting her elbows on the railing, as if settling in to listen to the proceedings.

'Look, signora, must we speak at this distance?' the inspector asked.

'I don't have a problem with it.'

'Well, I do have a problem with it. Come down to the porter's desk at once. I'll meet you there.'

He closed the little gate, got into his car, circled round the building, stopped in front of the main entrance, got out, climbed four steps, went inside, and found himself face to face with the concierge, who was getting out of the lift sideways, pulling in her tits and paunch as best she could. Once out, the ball re-inflated.

'Well?' she asked belligerently.

'I'd like to ask you a few questions about the Alfanos.'

'Them again? Haven't we heard enough about them? What's your rank in the police?'

'I'm an inspector.'

'Ah, well, then, can't you ask your colleague Macannuco about it instead of hassling me again? Do I have to keep repeating the same story to all the inspectors in the kingdom?'

'I think you mean the republic, signora.' Montalbano was starting to have fun.

'Never! I do not recognize this republic of shit! I am a monarchist and I'll die a monarchist!'

Montalbano smiled cheerfully, then assumed a conspiratorial air, looked around carefully, bent down towards the ball, and said in a low voice: 'I'm a monarchist, too, signora, but I can't say so openly, or else my career ... You understand.'

'My name is Esterina Trippodo,' the ball said, holding out a tiny, doll-like hand to him. 'Please come with me.'

They went down a flight of stairs and entered an apartment almost identical to the Alfanos'. On the right-hand wall in the entrance hall was a portrait of King Vittorio Emanuele III under a little lamp, which was lit. Next to this, lit up in turn, was a photo of his son, Umberto, who had been king for about a month, though Montalbano's memory was a bit hazy. On the left-hand wall, on the other hand, was a photograph, unlit, of another Vittorio Emanuele, Umberto's son, the one known in the scandal sheets for a stray shot he had once fired. The inspector looked at the photo in admiration.

'He certainly is a handsome man,' said Montalbano, bullshitter extraordinaire, without shame.

Esterina Trippodo brought her index finger to her lips, then applied her kiss to the photograph.

'Come in, come in, please make yourself at home.'

The kitchen–living room was ever so slightly bigger than the Alfanos'.

'Can I make you some coffee?' asked Esterina.

'Yes, thank you.'

As the lady was fumbling with the *napoletana*, Montalbano asked:

'Do you know the Alfanos?'

'Of course.'

'Did you see them the last time they were here, on the third and the fourth of September?'

Esterina launched into a monologue.

'No. But they were here, certainly. He's a gentleman. He called me to ask me to buy a bouquet of roses and to have them left outside the door to their apartment, and said they would be arriving in the early afternoon. He'd asked me to do this before. But that evening, the roses were still outside the door. The next day I dropped by a little before noon to pick up the money for the roses. The flowers were gone, but nobody answered the door. They'd already left. So I opened their gate – I'm the only

one's got a key – to empty the rubbish – it's my job –
but all I found in the bin was a syringe full of blood.
They didn't even put it in a bag or a piece of paper!
Nothing! Just thrown there! Disgusting! Lucky I had
gloves on! Who knows what the hell the slut was up to!'

'Did you mention these things to Inspector Macannuco?'

'No, why? He's not one of us!'

'What about the roses, were you paid for them?'

'Good things come to those who wait!'

'If I may presume ...' said Montalbano, reaching into
his wallet.

Mrs Trippodo magnanimously allowed him to presume.

'I noticed an electricity bill under the little table in
the entrance,' said the inspector.

'When the bills come, I slip them under the door.
Apparently she didn't take that one away with her and
pay it.'

And in the name of their common faith in the
monarchy, she answered all his other questions in gener-
ous detail.

*

Half an hour or so later, Montalbano got back in his car,
and after barely five minutes on the road, he saw the sign
for Palmi. It was logical, therefore, that Dolores had
taken this road instead of the autostrada. At once the

sign for the state road to Lido di Palmi appeared before him.

Jesus! It was barely two and a half miles from the apartment on Via Gerace! You could even walk there! Taking the state road, he spotted a motel barely a hundred yards later. If Dolores had her accident right at the state road, there was a very good chance this was the motel she went to.

He parked the car, got out, and went into the bar, which was also the motel's front desk. It was empty. Even the coffee machine was turned off.

'Anybody here?'

Behind a bead curtain that concealed a door on the left, a voice called out.

'I'll be right there!'

A man without a hint of hair on his head appeared, short, fat, ruddy, and likeable.

'Can I help you?'

'Hello, the name's Lojacano, I'm with the insurance company, and I need a little information from you, if you'd be so kind. And who are you, if I may ask?'

'I'm Rocco Sudano, I own this place. But at the moment, since it's the low season, I take care of almost everything myself.'

'Listen, was your motel open on this past September the fourth?'

'Of course. That's still high season.'

'Were you here?'

'Yes.'

'Do you remember whether that morning, a dark, very attractive woman came in after having a minor accident on the state road?'

Rocco Sudano's eyes started glistening, and even his billiard-ball head started glowing as if there were a lamp inside it. His mouth broadened into a smile of contentment.

'I certainly do remember! How could I forget? Signora Dolores!' Then, suddenly worried: 'Has something happened to her?'

'No, nothing. As I said, I'm with the insurance company. It's about the accident she had, remember?'

'Yes, of course.'

'Do you recollect by any chance what the lady did for the rest of that day?'

'Well, yes. You don't see a whole lot of women like that, not even in high season! First she went to her room and rested for a couple of hours. She wasn't hurt or anything, just very scared. I even brought her some camomile tea, and she was lying down . . .'

He lost himself in the memory, a dreamy look in his eyes, and, without realizing, started licking his lips. Montalbano snapped him out of it.

'Do you remember what time of day she arrived?'

'Uh, it must've been ten, ten-thirty.'

'And what did she do next?'

'She ate in our restaurant, which was still open then,

being high season. Then she came down and said she was going to the beach. I saw her again in the evening, but she didn't have dinner here. She went to her room. At seven o'clock the next morning Silvestro, the mechanic, brought her car back. And then she paid and left.'

'One last question. Are there any buses or private coaches linking Lido di Palmi and Gioia Tauro?'

'Yes, in the high season. There's a number of transportation services, which also go further than just Gioia Tauro and Palmi, naturally.'

'So they were probably still running on September the fourth, right?'

'Around here, the high season lasts until the end of September.'

Montalbano looked at his watch. It was gone five.

'Listen, Mr Sudano, I need to rest for a couple of hours. Have you got any rooms available?'

'Any one you want. It's low season.'

FIFTEEN

He slept like a log for four hours straight. When he woke up, he called Fazio on his mobile phone.

'I'm not going to make it back tonight. I'll see you tomorrow morning at the station.'

'All right, Chief.'

'Did you talk to Alfano's friend?'

'Yes.'

'Did he tell you anything interesting?'

'Yes.'

It must be really interesting, if the words had to be dragged out of Fazio's mouth. Whenever he had something decisive to tell him about a case, he only revealed it in dribs and drabs.

'What did he say?'

'He said that what got Arturo Pecorini to move so suddenly out of Vigàta was the Sinagras.'

Montalbano balked.

'The Sinagras?!'

'Yes indeed, Chief. Don Balduccio himself.'

'And what was the reason?'

'Because rumours were starting to circulate in town about an affair between the butcher and Signora Dolores. So Don Balduccio sent word to Pecorini that it was best if he had a change of scene.'

'I see.'

'By the way, Chief, Prosecutor Tommaseo was looking for you.'

'Do you know what he wanted?'

'He talked to Catarella, so who knows. From what I could gather, he said a colleague of his from Reggio had called about a disappearance. He complained that he didn't know anything about the case. He wants to be filled in. I think Tommaseo's colleague was referring to our very own Giovanni Alfano.'

'I think so, too. I'll go and talk to him tomorrow.'

The inspector got out of bed, showered, changed his clothes, and went to the front desk in the bar. Mr Sudano didn't want to be paid ('It's low season, after all').

He got in the car and left.

When he got to Villa San Giovanni it was already past ten. He headed for the trattoria where he had eaten at midday. And he wasn't disappointed the fourth time, either.

At one o'clock in the morning he was back in Sicily.

He travelled down the road between Messina and

Catania under a sort of rough copy of the Great Flood. The windscreen wipers were helpless to wipe away the heavens' waters. He stopped at the Autogrill service areas at Barracca, Calatabiano, and Aci Sant'Antonio, to fill up more on courage than on coffee. When all was said and done, it had taken him three hours to drive a distance that would have taken an hour and a half in normal weather. But once he'd left Catania behind and got on the autostrada for Enna, the deluge not only stopped suddenly, but the stars came out. Taking the Mulinello state road, he headed in the direction of Nicosia. Half an hour later, he saw on the right a sign for Mascalippa. He took that road, a dilapidated mess that here and there still preserved a faded memory of tarmac. As he entered Mascalippa, there wasn't a living soul in the streets. He stopped in the town square, which was exactly the same as he had left it so many years before, got out of the car, and lit a cigarette. The cold penetrated straight to the bones, and the air smelled of grass and straw. A dog approached him, then stopped short a few steps away, wagging its tail in friendship.

'Come here, Argos,' said Montalbano.

The dog looked at him, turned around, and sauntered off.

'Argos!' he called again.

But the dog vanished round a corner. It was right. It knew it wasn't Argos. The idiot was him, pretending to be Ulysses. He finished his cigarette, got back in his car, and began the journey home to Vigàta.

*

He awoke after a good sleep, calm and untroubled. On the road from Mascalippa, his mind had cleared up, and he now knew what he had to do. He phoned Livia before she left for work. At nine o'clock he called Dr Lattes, the chief of the commissioner's cabinet. And he arrived at the station fresh, rested, and serene, as if he had got a full night's sleep. Whereas, in fact, he had slept barely three hours.

'Ahh, Chief, Chief! Yest'day Proseccotor Gommaseo called 'n' said—'

'I know already, Fazio told me. Is he in his office?'

'Who? Gommaseo?'

'No, Fazio.'

'Yessir.'

'Send him to me at once.'

Lots of newly arrived mail, gobs of it, covered the whole desktop. He sat down and pushed the envelopes to the far edges to create a bit of space in front of him – not for writing anything, but for resting his elbows.

Fazio came in.

'Close the door, sit down, and tell me the story of Balduccio Sinagra and Pecorini again, in fuller detail.'

'Chief, you told me to talk to Giovanni Alfano's third friend, remember? Well, it was this friend, whose name is

Franco Di Gregorio, and who seems like a decent man, who told me the whole story.'

'But the other two didn't even mention it to me.'

'They didn't want to talk about it.'

'And why not?'

'If you'll let me tell it my way, I'll get to that.'

'All right, go on.'

'Let's just say that over two years ago, this fifty-year-old butcher falls head over heels for Dolores Alfano, who used to buy her meat from him. But he doesn't go about it under cover, on the sly – nosirree, he starts sending her a bouquet of roses every morning, buys her gifts, sweets, and even fancy things, plants himself outside her home, waiting for her to come out so he can follow behind her ... In short, the whole town finds out about it.'

'Is he married?'

'No, he's not.'

'But doesn't he know that Dolores is Alfano's wife, and that Alfano is Balduccio's protégé?'

'He does, he does.'

'Then he's a fool!'

'No, Chief, he's not a fool. He's a cocky, violent man. The kind who says he's not afraid of anything or anyone.'

'A windbag?'

'No, sir. Arturo Pecorini is a man who doesn't mess around. He's a thug. When he was barely twenty years old he was arrested for murder, then acquitted for lack of evidence. Five years later, another acquittal, for attempted murder. After that there are no more serious offences, aside from a few fights, since he is a bully, after all. When friends tell him he should be more careful with this Dolores business, he replies that he doesn't give a shit about the Sinagras. He says, let 'em try and they'll see.'

'And why didn't Dolores go to the carabinieri the way she did with the other lovesick suitor?'

Fazio grinned.

'Di Gregorio says she didn't do anything because she actually liked the butcher. A lot, in fact.'

'Were they lovers?'

'Nobody can say for certain. But bear in mind that the butcher lived, and still lives, barely twenty yards from the Alfanos. At night they could do as they pleased; the roads around there have hardly any traffic in the daytime, so imagine at night. But then the story reached Don Balduccio's ears, and he wasn't at all pleased to hear that the butcher was cuckolding a distant relative of his, a young man he was particularly fond of.'

'What did he do?'

'The first thing he did was call Dolores.'

'What did he say to her?'

'Nobody knows. But Di Gregorio says you can imagine. And he's right. In fact, four days later, Dolores left for Colombia, telling everyone she was going to see her mother, who was unwell.'

'And what about Pecorini?'

'Chief, I'm going to preface this the same way Di

Gregorio did for me: this is all only gossip, conjecture, surmise.'

'Let's hear it anyway.'

'Pecorini, when he was twenty, raped a seventeen-year-old girl, the daughter of very poor parents. Pecorini's father paid the girl's family off, and in return they didn't report it. But the girl got pregnant. And brought a little boy into the world. Who was called Arturo, like his father, and Manzella, like his mother. And, as these things go, Pecorini became fond of his unacknowledged son, helped him to study, get his diploma, and find a job. He's thirty years old now, with a degree in accounting, married and with a three-year-old little boy, Carmelo.'

'Hold on, Fazio! What is this, the Bible?'

'We're almost there, Chief. One day, when the kid was playing outside the front door of their building, he disappeared.'

'What do you mean, "disappeared"?'

'Disappeared, Chief. Vanished. Twenty-four hours later, Arturo Pecorini shut down his shop and left for Catania.'

'And what about the kid?'

'Thirty-six hours later, he was found playing outside the front door of his building.'

'And what'd he say?'

'He said a nice old gentleman, a grandfatherly sort, asked him if he wanted to go for a ride and took him in his car to a beautiful house with many toys inside. Three

229

days later he left him in the same place he'd picked him up.'

'That's Balduccio's style, all right. The old man wanted to carry out the operation himself. Then what happened?'

'Pecorini had got the drift of Balduccio's signals and moved out. And so Dolores was allowed to return. But Giovanni Alfano's friends were approached by some of the Sinagra family's men, and they were all given the same advice: not to mention this business about the butcher to Giovanni when he returned, because Don Balduccio didn't want him to get upset.'

'But last time you told me that nowadays Pecorini can come back to town every so often.'

'Yes, he comes for two days a week, Saturdays and Sundays. A short while after he moved to Catania he reopened his shop here and put his brother in charge of it. They say he's completely over Dolores now.'

'All right, then, thanks.'

'Chief, would you explain to me how you knew that the butcher had had an affair with Dolores Alfano?'

'But I didn't know!'

'Oh, no? Then how come you immediately started asking me for information about Pecorini? Even before Dolores first came to the station!'

He couldn't tell him the real reason – that is, that the butcher owned the house where Mimì was performing gymnastics with Dolores.

'Maybe one day I'll tell you, or you'll work it out yourself. Do you know if Inspector Augello is in his office?'

'Yes, he is. Shall I go and get him for you?'

'Yes. And come back with him.'

Fazio went out. Montalbano leaned back in his chair, closed his eyes, and took two or three deep breaths, as if about to dive underwater. The scene he had in mind had to come out perfectly, without one word too many or too few. He heard them approaching. He kept his eyes closed. He looked rapt in meditation.

'Mimì, come in and sit down. Fazio, go and tell Catarella I don't want to be disturbed for any reason, then come back.'

He still had his eyes closed and Mimì said nothing. He heard Fazio's footsteps returning.

'Come in, lock the door behind you, and sit down.'

At last he opened his eyes. It had been several days since he last saw Mimì. His face was yellow and unshaven, his eyes hollow, his clothes wrinkled. He sat on the edge of the chair and kept the heel of his right foot raised, nervously shaking his leg. He seemed tight as a rope that might snap at any moment. Fazio, for his part, looked worried.

'Lately,' Montalbano began, 'the air we've been breathing in this department hasn't been very good.'

'I'd like to explain—'

'Mimì, you'll talk when I say you can. Most probably the responsibility for what has been happening is largely my own. I – and I'm the first to realize this – no longer have the energy and confidence that used to have you all following my lead, always and no matter what. We had become more than a team; we were a single body. But then the head of this body stopped working so well, and the whole body started feeling the effects. As the saying goes, a fish always starts rotting at the head.'

'But, Salvo—'

'I still haven't given you permission to speak, Mimì . . . It's therefore natural that some part of this body should refuse to decay with the rest. I'm referring to you, Mimì. But before saying what I feel I must say to you, I contest your assertion that I have never wanted to grant you any autonomy, any leeway for making your own decisions. Stop, no talking. On the contrary, as Fazio can attest, I have been trying, especially lately, to unload practically every investigation on you, precisely because I felt, and feel, that I'm no longer the man I used to be. And if that hasn't been the case as often as I would have liked, it's because of your family commitments, Mimì. I've taken on certain investigations to leave you more time to devote to your family. And now you ask me, in writing, to assign you the case of the *critaru* murder. Are you getting ready to take over for me, Mimì?'

'May I speak?'

'Only to answer my question.'

'The situation is not what you think.'

'Then you don't need to explain anything else to me.

I think what I say will be enough for you. You don't need a written reply. OK.'

'What do you mean, "OK"?'

'The Skorpio case is yours, Inspector Callahan.'

Mimì gave him a bewildered look. He hadn't understood Montalbano's cinematic allusion. Fazio did, however, and immediately turned red in the face.

'You mean you're passing it off?'

'Exactly.'

Mimì finally caught on.

'You're giving me the case?'

'Yes.'

'Are you sure? You're not going to regret it later on?'

'I'm not going to regret it.'

'And you won't interfere in the investigation?'

'No.'

'I'll have complete freedom of action?'

'Of course.'

'And what do you want in exchange?'

'Mimì, we're not at the market. All I want is for you to respect the rules.'

'Meaning?'

'That, before taking any step whatsoever – arrests, press conferences, public declarations – you will inform me first.'

'And what if you tell me not to do it?'

'I won't. You can be sure of it. I only want to be informed daily on the developments of the case.'

'All right, then. Thanks.'

Mimì stood up and held out his hand to him. Montalbano took it and squeezed it rather tight. Mimì couldn't resist any longer.

'May I embrace you?' he asked.

'Of course.'

They embraced. Mimì's eyes were moist.

'This morning I phoned Dr Lattes,' said the inspector. 'Today is Wednesday, and this evening I'm leaving for Boccadasse to see Livia. I'll be away until Sunday. So you have to replace me in every respect, Mimì. Fazio will now go into your office and explain to you how far we've got on the case. And he'll put himself at your disposal. As soon as you can, call Tommaseo and bring him up to speed on everything. Fazio'll be with you in three minutes.'

Mimì went out looking so happy, he seemed he might start dancing at any moment.

'He looked like he was about to kiss your hand,' Fazio said disparagingly. 'And now, would you please explain to me why you had this brilliant idea?'

'Because I'm tired.'

'Come on, you can't be *that* tired. I don't believe it.'

'Well, then, it's because I can't stand this investigation any longer.'

'Oh, yeah? When did you reach your breaking point? Yesterday at Gioia Tauro?'

'Well, then, it's because Mimì deserves it.'

'No, sir, Mimì does not deserve it.'

'Fazio, can we put a little distance back between the two of us? I decided to do this because I felt like it. And I don't feel like discussing it any longer.'

'Look, Chief, he's going to send the department to hell in a hand basket. He's not right in the head. I don't know what's got into him. And this is a delicate matter, with the Mafia smack dab in the middle. I don't want to work with Inspector Augello.'

'Fazio, it's not a question of what you want or don't want. It's an order.'

Fazio stood up, pale as a corpse and stiff as a broomstick.

'Yes, sir.'

'Wait. Try to understand. It's precisely because it's such a delicate matter, as you said, that I want you working alongside Augello.'

'Chief, if he takes off like a rocket, I'm certainly not going to be able to stop him.'

'If you alert me in time, I'll step in.'

'But you'll be in Boccadasse!'

'I don't think anything will happen in these next three days. In any case I'll take my mobile phone. And don't you have Livia's home phone number?'

*

He didn't feel the least bit guilty leaving his mobile phone at home in Marinella, actually hiding it in the drawer

ANDREA CAMILLERI

where he kept his clean linen. That way poor Fazio, too, at the right moment, would get his own taste of betrayal. This was the first time Montalbano had ever told him one thing while secretly intending to do another. It was, moreover, inevitable: Weren't they all treading in the potter's field now?

*

He retraced the same route as the day before, but this time he didn't slow down to take in the landscape. At the junction for Catania, instead of turning towards the airport, he continued straight towards the town centre. A short while later he found himself caught in a traffic jam that slowed him down to barely five miles per hour, which was too slow even for him, not to mention the repeated jams that lasted a good ten minutes each time. During one of these stops a traffic policeman passed his car.

'Excuse me, but, what's going on?'
'Where?'
'Here. Why is there all this traffic?'
'You call this traffic?' said the policeman, surprised.

Which meant that this was perfectly normal. By the grace of God he came at last within view of the arcades of the port district. He asked where customs was, and as he was heading there, he drove slowly past three sparkling display windows full of meat, exhibited the way jewels used to be at Bulgari's. A big, lit-up sign said: PECORINI

— THE KING OF MEAT. Finding a legal parking space was, of course, a fantasy, and so he stopped the car inside a sort of great open doorway with its door unhinged and got out.

At Pecorini's, the similarity with the display windows at Bulgari's was heightened by the prices accompanying the different cuts of meat.

As he entered the shop he felt as if he was entering the reception room of a first-class beauty salon. Sofas, armchairs, little tables. As there was a group of people at the very elegant counter, he sat down in an armchair, and at once a girl of about eighteen appeared dressed as a waitress, in starched cap and apron.

'Would you like a coffee?'

'No, thank you. There are too many people. I'll come back later.'

As he stood up, the man at the cash register looked up and eyed him.

In a flash, Montalbano was sure of two things: one, that the man was Arturo Pecorini and, two, that Pecorini had recognized him, because he had frozen in the act of giving change to a customer. Perhaps he had seen the inspector on television.

＊

After parking the car at the airport, Montalbano broke into a sprint, as there were only twenty minutes left before take-off. Glancing at a monitor to see what gate the flight was leaving from, he saw only a blank. He looked more closely: the flight would be leaving with a delay of an hour and a half. And this, too, was perfectly normal, just like the traffic.

SIXTEEN

After they'd had breakfast together, Livia went to the office. Left alone, Montalbano unplugged the telephone, dawdled about the apartment for an hour or so, then showered, dressed, and spent another hour smoking and gazing at the landscape through Livia's big picture window. Then he left Boccadasse and went into Genoa. He went to the Aquarium and, after a half-hour wait in the queue, managed to get in. He spent the rest of the morning among the fish, charmed and bemused. At lunchtime he went to a trattoria that Livia had recommended. In every place he'd ever been in his life, he had always adapted to the local cuisine. He was sure that if he ever ended up in the godforsaken mountains of Afghanistan, a waiter would say to him something like: 'We have an excellent dish of worms with a side helping of fried cockroaches,' and he would confidently accept.

This time the waiter asked him: 'Pesto?'

ANDREA CAMILLERI

'Of course,' he replied.

But when the waiter listed the main dishes for him, which were all fish, Montalbano felt it wasn't right to eat them after seeing all those beautiful, living fish at the Aquarium.

'Could I have a veal *alla milanese*?'

'Of course, if you go to Milan,' the waiter replied.

He ended up eating an excellent fried sole, begging forgiveness. Back in Boccadasse, he lay down in bed. He woke up around four o'clock, got out of bed and went back to the picture window to read the newspaper he had bought. Dress rehearsal for life in retirement, he thought to himself, half amused, half dejected.

Livia came home at six.

'You know what? When I told my friend Laura you were here, she invited us to spend the weekend at her villa in Portofino. Feel like going?'

'But I have to be back in Vigàta by Sunday evening.'

'Let's do this. We can leave tomorrow morning, spend all of Saturday there and then, Sunday morning, after breakfast, I'll drive you to the airport.'

'OK.'

'Why did you unplug the telephone?'

'Because I didn't want to be bothered by any calls from Vigàta.'

Livia looked at him in shock.

'You used to fret when you had no news from Fazio or Mimì. Do you realize you've changed?'

'Yes,' he admitted.

*

They went out to eat at the trattoria the inspector had chosen as the Boccadassian alternative to the Vigatese Enzo's. Before the food arrived, Livia brought up the subject of Mimì. She was worried.

'When was the last time Beba called you?'

'Three days ago.'

'You'll see, the next time she calls she'll tell you things are going better with Mimì.'

'Have the stake-outs ended?'

'Not yet, unfortunately. But since I know the commissioner is going to commend him for his work, his mood will definitely change, you'll see.'

Is it possible that one never ends telling lies in life?

*

He got back to Vigàta at nine in the evening, went to eat at Enzo's, and was home in Marinella by ten-thirty. He undressed, sat down in the armchair, and turned on the television. The Free Channel was running its umpteenth programme on the arrival of illegal immigrants on Italian shores. TeleVigàta, for its part, featured the thousandth round-table discussion on the construction of the bridge over the Straits of Messina. As there was still half an hour to go before the night-time news broadcasts, he went for a walk along the beach.

On his way back, he thought he heard the telephone ring. He didn't run to pick it up. It couldn't have been Livia, since he'd phoned her from the trattoria. Surely it was Fazio. Once inside, he turned the television back on and tuned in to TeleVigàta. He was more than certain that during his absence Mimì had taken some initiative of his own and Fazio hadn't been able to inform him in time because there was no way to reach him in Boccadasse. And, indeed, the news he was expecting was the first item on the programme.

'Major new developments are expected in the case of the man whose dismembered body was found at the so-called *critaru*,' the newsreader began.

Then, in order of importance, he ran through the other headlines of the stories he would cover during the broadcast – fatal crashes on the Montelusa–Palermo highway; sheep stolen in Fela; robbery of a supermarket in Fiacca; a three-year-old boy who fell from a fourth-floor balcony in Montelusa and was unharmed thanks, according to his mother, to the miraculous intervention of Padre Pio; two regional deputies arrested for collusion with the Mafia – before returning to the first story, which featured footage of *'u critaru* itself; of Pasquale Ajena, the owner, showing the place where he had first seen the bag with the corpse inside; of the beautiful Dolores Alfano in tears, being supported by Prosecutor Tommaseo, who couldn't hide his pleasure at putting his hands all over those gifts from God; of Mimì in glory and triumph displaying something tiny that Montalbano only afterwards realized was the famous bridge that Alfano had swallowed; of Fazio performing an acrobatic leap to get out of shot.

The essence of the news reported by the newsreader boiled down to the fact that Dolores had been unable to identify the corpse, 'though she knew in her heart of hearts that the meagre remains must belong to her husband'. He added that it would soon be possible to identify him through DNA testing, since samples of his blood had been taken by the forensics laboratory of the Reggio Calabria police from the traces found in the victim's apartment in Gioia Tauro. In fact, Dolores Alfano recalled that on the morning her husband failed to board his ship, he had cut himself while shaving with a straight razor. This surprised Montalbano. He hadn't seen any blood in the bathroom of the Via Gerace apartment, either in the photos or in person. Perhaps Forensics had cleaned it all up. At the end of the news report, it was time for the editorial of Pippo Ragonese, the purse-lipped prince of opinion at TeleVigàta.

'Just a few words to underscore how clear it is to everyone that as soon as the investigation into the *critaru* murder was passed on from Inspector Montalbano to his second-in-command, Inspector Domenico Augello, it immediately took a great leap forward. Indeed, in the space of barely more than twenty-four hours, Inspector Augello, under the guidance of Prosecutor Tommaseo, was able to identify with almost absolute certainty the man so brutally murdered. It must be said that in this particular case it was the close collaboration between Public Prosecutor Tommaseo and his counterpart in Reggio Calabria that yielded such impressive results. Inspector Augello also brought to our attention how the methods of the murder revived certain old Mafia rituals believed to have fallen into disuse. While he preferred not to name any names, it is obvious that the brilliant young deputy inspector already has a clear idea of who might be behind this. Whatever the case, we extend our heartfelt best wishes to Inspector Augello and fervently hope that Inspector Montalbano continues to refrain from participating in this investigation.

'And now let us move on to the arrest of two regional parliamentary deputies of the Centre-Right on suspicion of collusion with the Mafia. While we have, of course, only the deepest respect for the magistrature, we cannot help but note that it moves all too often in only one direction. Is it possible, we ask as honest citizens, that—'

Montalbano turned it off. Everything had gone exactly as expected. He hadn't missed a beat. He had started a game of chess and made the first move (truth be told, he'd had Mimì, the unwitting player, make it). He should have felt satisfied, but he didn't. He felt ashamed of the way he was acting, but it was the only course of action he had come up with. Now all that remained for him to do was to pretend to be angry at Mimì and wait for the person who was supposed to make the next move to make it. Because someone, upon hearing Ragonese's words, was going to feel dragged into this case, and would react accordingly. Which would be the second move of the game.

The phone rang. It was Fazio.

'Ah, finally, Chief! I tried calling you about an hour ago and—'

'I heard the phone ringing but didn't pick up in time.'

'Did you watch the news?'

'Yes.'

'Chief, you have no idea how many times I tried to reach you in Boccadasse to warn you that Inspector Augello was—'

'I believe you, I believe you. Like an idiot I left my mobile phone here, and in Boccadasse I was always out of the house. I'm very sorry, it's all my fault.'

'You should know that early tomorrow morning Augello is meeting Prosecutor Tommaseo and the commissioner.'

'Let them have their meeting, and get a good night's sleep. Oh, and listen. Did Mimì somehow find out I went to Gioia Tauro?'

'No. Who would've told him?'

*

Augello returned to the station late in the morning. He didn't look very pleased with his meeting in Montelusa.

'Mimì, what the hell have you been cooking up?'

'Me?!'

'Yes, you. Last night I watched Ragonese on TV. I told you I wanted to be informed of every move you made.'

'But, Salvo, how was I going to inform you if you weren't here? Anyway, what did I say or do that was new? All I did was relate to Tommaseo what Fazio filled me in on.'

'Namely?'

'That you thought the *critaru* body belonged to Dolores Alfano's husband, and that he'd been killed by the Mafia for being a courier who had betrayed the family. Not one word more or less than that.'

The inspector should have embraced and thanked Mimì, but he couldn't.

'But you also told the journalists.'

'I had Tommaseo's authorization to do so.'

'Well, OK. How did your meeting go this morning?'

'Badly.'

'Why?'

'Because Tommaseo wants to proceed very cautiously with Balduccio Sinagra. He says we have nothing against him at the moment. But I say how can that be? Isn't Balduccio Sinagra a Mafia thug and a killer?'

'So what, Mimì? It's true he's a killer, but what if he

didn't kill Alfano? Do you still want to pin the murder on him anyway? Are you saying that one murder more, one murder less, makes no difference? Well, I've got news for you: it does.'

'So now you're defending him?'

Montalbano had a flash. He suddenly remembered the nightmare he'd had a few nights before, when Totò Riina had offered him the post of Minister of the Interior.

'Mimì, don't talk crap,' he said, though in his mind the words were directed at Riina. 'I'm not defending a Mafioso, I'm telling you to be careful about accusing some-one, Mafioso or no, of a crime he cannot have committed.'

'I'm convinced he had Alfano killed.'

'Then try to convince Tommaseo. Where does the commissioner stand on this?'

'He agrees with Tommaseo. But he suggested I talk to Musante.'

'I don't think he'll be of any help to you. How are Beba and the boy doing?'

'Fine.'

Mimì got up to leave, but Montalbano stopped him before he could open the door.

'I'm sorry, Mimì, but I've been wanting to ask you something for a long time, and since lately we haven't had any chance to talk, I—'

'Go ahead.'

'Do you know anything about three men from Cata-nia...' He broke off, opened the top drawer on the left of his desk, grabbed the first sheet of paper that came within reach, and pretended to read: '... whose names are Bonura, Pecorini, and Di Silvestro?'

Having uttered the question, Montalbano felt poised on the edge of a cliff. He stared at Mimì with both eyes pointed at him like shotgun barrels and hoped that what he felt inside didn't show on his face. The first and third names he had invented. Mimì looked genuinely befuddled.

'Wait a second. I think I remember a certain Di Silvestro we dealt with last year, though I can't remember why. The other two I've never heard of before. Why, are they of interest to you?'

'They came up a while ago in a case of attempted murder I was investigating. But that's all right, it's not important. I'll be seeing you.'

It was an extremely risky question to ask, but he was glad he had asked it. If Mimì had said he knew Pecorini, then his position, in Montalbano's eyes, would have been seriously compromised. Dolores therefore must not have told him about her affair with the butcher. All things considered, it wouldn't have been in her interests. More importantly, she also had not told him that the house where they had their amorous encounters belonged to Pecorini. The inspector felt so pleased that he surprised himself whistling, something he'd never known how to do.

*

The second move he had been expecting was made late that evening, just as he was heading to the bathroom to get undressed for bed.

'Inspector Montalbano?'

'Speaking.'

'I am terribly embarrassed to have to phone you at this hour, disturbing you in the intimacy of your home, probably after a long day of hard work . . .'

The inspector immediately recognized the voice at the other end of the line. It wasn't just the voice, but the manner of speaking, the flowery phrases, that gave him away. Still, he had to play along.

'Could you please tell me who I'm speaking to?'

'I am Orazio Guttadauro, the lawyer.'

The very first time he'd had any dealings with Guttadauro, it had seemed to him that a worm had a keener sense of honesty than this lawyer, who was Don Balduccio Sinagra's right-hand man. And after getting to know him a little, he had become convinced that a pile of dog-shit had a keener sense of honesty.

'Good evening, sir! And how is your friend and client?'

There was no need to mention any names. Guttadauro heaved a tortured sigh, then another. And then he spoke.

'It's so sad, dear Inspector, so sad!'

'He's not well?'

'I don't know whether you're aware that he was very ill a few months ago.'

'I've heard it mentioned.'

'Then he recovered somewhat, at least physically, thank God.'

Montalbano asked himself a subtle theological question: Should God be thanked for letting a multiple murderer like Balduccio get better?

'Sometimes, however,' the lawyer continued, 'he's no longer all there in the head. His moments of lucidity alternate with moments of, well, confusion, lapses of memory ... It's so sad, Inspector! A great mind like that!'

Should he join in the lament? He decided against it. Nor should he even ask the reason for the telephone call.

'Well, Mr Guttadauro, I wish you a good night and—'

'Inspector, I must ask you a favour on behalf of my client and friend.'

'If I can.'

'He so wishes to see you. He told me that before closing his eyes for ever he would really, and I mean really, like to meet you one more time. You are aware of the high esteem in which he holds you. He says that men of exemplary honesty such as yourself should ...'

... *become Minister of the Interior*, thought Montalbano. But instead he said: 'Certainly, one of these days ...'

'No, Inspector, I'm afraid I haven't made myself clear. He would like to see you immediately.'

'Now?!'

'Now. You know what old people are like. They

become very stubborn and whimsical. Please don't disappoint the poor old man ... If you open your front door, you'll find a car waiting for you. All you have to do is get in. We are waiting for you. I'll look forward to seeing you shortly.'

They hung up simultaneously. They had managed to talk for fifteen minutes without uttering the name of Balduccio Sinagra. The inspector put on his jacket and opened the door. In the darkness the car, which must have been black, was not visible. But its engine, which was running, was purring like a cat.

*

The lawyer opened the car door for him, showed him into the villa, and led him all the way to Don Balduccio's bedroom. It was outfitted like a hospital room, and it smelled of medication. The old man lay in bed with his eyes closed; he had oxygen tubes in his nostrils, and there was a huge tank at the head of the bed. Beside the tank stood a man nearly six and a half feet tall, a sort of wardrobe with legs. Guttadauro leaned over the old man and whispered a few words to him. Don Balduccio opened his eyes and extended a transparent hand to Montalbano. Who shook it ever so lightly, afraid that if he shook it any harder it would break like glass. Then Don Balduccio made a sign to the human wardrobe. Who, in the twinkling of an eye, turned a handle that tilted the bed slightly and raised Don Balduccio to a sitting position; then he arranged some pillows behind the old man's back, removed the tubes from his nose, closed the oxygen tank, put a chair very close to the bed, and left.

The lawyer remained standing, leaning against a set of shelves.

'I can't read any more,' Don Balduccio began, 'my eyesight's failing. An' so I have the papers read to me. 'Parently in the States the number of executions from the death penalty is up to a thousand.'

'Right,' said the worldly Montalbano, showing no surprise at the don's starting the conversation with such a subject.

'One was granted a reprieve,' Guttadauro interjected. 'But they quickly made up for this by killing another man in another state.'

'Are you for or against it, Inspector?' asked the old man.

'I'm against capital punishment,' said Montalbano.

'I would never have doubted it in a man like you. I'm against it, too.'

What? Against it? Hadn't he condemned to death the ten or more people he'd had killed? Or did Don Balduccio differentiate between deaths ordered by him and those ordered by the state?

'But I used to be in favour,' the old man added.

Now his statement made more sense. How many hit men had he kept on his payroll in the past?

'Then I realized my mistake, because there's no

remedy for death. I became convinced of this by something that happened, many years ago . . . to a relative of mine . . . in Colombia . . . Orazio, my friend, would you give me a glass of water?'

Guttadauro served him.

'You have to forgive me, talking makes me very tired . . . I was told that this relative . . . was pursuing his own interests . . . instead of mine . . . I believed it, and I made a mistake . . . I gave a wrong order . . . Do you follow?'

'Perfectly.'

'I was younger, and I didn't think before I acted . . . Not six months later, I found out that the things I was told about that man weren't true . . . But I'd already made my mistake . . . There was no turning back . . . How could I make up for it? There was only one way. To make his son my son. And let him have a clean life. An' this kid loved me despite . . . and would never have done me . . . a bad turn . . . never done nothing . . . to displ . . . displease me . . . I can't talk . . . no more.'

He stopped. It was clear he was running completely out of breath.

'Would you like me to continue?' Guttadauro asked.

'Yes. But first . . .'

'Yes, of course. Gnazio!'

The wardrobe appeared instantly. There was no need for words. The giant lowered the bed, removed a pillow, slipped the tubes back into the old man's nostrils, reopened the oxygen tank, and went out.

Then Guttadauro continued.

'Before going back to board his ship, Giovanni Alfano — who, you will have understood, is the person we're talking about — came here with his wife to say goodbye to Don Balduccio.'

'Yes, I know. Signora Dolores showed me the photographs.'

'Good. On that occasion, Don Balduccio called Giovanni aside to give him something. A letter. To be delivered in person to a friend in Villa San Giovanni, who would be waiting for him at an appointed place. And he begged him not to tell anyone about that letter, not even his wife.'

'And what happened?'

'Only about ten days ago, Don Balduccio learned that this letter was never delivered.'

'Why did it take so long to find out?'

'Well! First there was my friend's illness, then the long convalescence, then the person who was supposed to have received the letter had an accident and was unable to get in touch with us . . . He was shot three times, but by mistake, you know . . . by someone who has remained anonymous . . .'

'I see. Was it an important letter?'

'Very important,' the old man said from deep in his bed.

'And did you tell Alfano how important it was?'

'Yes,' said Don Balduccio.

'Could you tell me what it said?'

Guttadauro didn't answer right away, but looked over at Don Balduccio, who nodded yes.

'You know, Inspector, Don Balduccio has a very wide range of business interests . . . The letter contained – how shall I put it – instructions, if you will, concerning a possible agreement with some of our business competitors in Calabria . . .'

A nice little pact between the Mafia and the 'Ndrangheta, in short.

'But why didn't you just post it?'

A strange noise came from the bed, a series of *hi hi* sounds halfway between sneezes and drunken hiccups. Montalbano realized the old man was laughing.

SEVENTEEN

'Post it? You surprise me,' said the lawyer. 'As you know, my friend has been the target of real and personal persecution by the police and the judiciary for many years. They intercept his letters, perform surprise searches, arrest him for no plausible reason ... They carry out acts of terrorism on him, that's the word.'

'And what, in your opinion, was the reason this letter was never delivered?'

'In our opinion, Giovanni wasn't able to deliver it.'

'Why not?'

'Because, in all probability, Giovanni never crossed the straits.'

'And where do you think he stopped?'

'We think he got no farther than Catania.'

So that was how things had gone, according to Balduccio and Guttadauro.

'But you ... why haven't you been busy trying to find

out what happened? Don Balduccio has many friends, he could easily have—'

'You see, Inspector, the point was not to find out what happened . . . Don Balduccio knew it intuitively . . . He told me everything as if he had been there himself . . . It's extraordinary . . . If anything, it was only a matter of confirming his intuition.'

'All right, but it amounts to the same thing: why didn't you seek out this confirmation?'

'Shit . . . is not something . . . I touch with my hands,' the old man said with difficulty.

Guttadauro the lawyer translated this for him. 'Don Balduccio felt that it was a matter for the law to handle.'

'So I was supposed to pick up the shit with my own hands?'

Guttadauro shrugged. 'It's what we were hoping. However, at that point, you stepped back and put your deputy into the mix,' he said.

'Who is making . . . big . . . mistake,' the old man chimed in.

'But we can't let him continue with his mistake for very long,' the lawyer said by way of conclusion.

'I'm very tired,' said Don Balduccio, closing his eyes.

Montalbano stood up and left the room, followed by Guttadauro.

'I didn't like your last statement one bit,' the inspector said harshly.

'I didn't either, having said it,' the lawyer replied. 'But

don't take it as a threat. Don Balduccio doesn't know yet, because I asked that he was not told, but I know.'

'Know what?'

'That your deputy and Dolores have been . . . well, let's say "meeting". It is in everyone's best interests that this affair ends as soon as possible.'

He showed him to his car, opened the door for him, closed it when Montalbano got in, and bowed when the car drove off.

*

It was late, but the inspector didn't feel the least bit like sleeping. He had a lot of thinking to do. Going into the kitchen, he prepared the usual six-cup pot of coffee. So Guttadauro knew about Dolores and Mimì. And the lawyer had given him a sort of deadline that was no joking matter. How would Balduccio react if he found out about the love affair between his adoptive daughter-in-law and the deputy inspector who was investigating him? Badly, no doubt. Because he would be convinced that Mimì was working in Dolores's favour. He would never believe that Mimì was acting in good faith. And the whole thing might take a dangerous turn. The coffee bubbled up. Montalbano poured himself a bowlful and sipped it slowly. Sitting out on the veranda was out of the question, as it was too cold, and so he sat down at the small dining-room table, paper and pen within reach. So what, in essence, had Balduccio told him? First of all, the old man had made a genuine confession to him — that is, he had Filippo Alfano killed in Colombia, convinced that Alfano had betrayed him. He had put himself in Montalbano's hands by admitting to the murder. But surely Balduccio had made that confession for a second purpose. What? The inspector wrote:

Find out when and how Filippo Alfano was murdered. Have Catarella do a search.

Secondly — and this was very important — the old man had told him that, realizing his mistake, he had taken it upon himself to care for Giovanni, Filippo's son, supporting his studies and making sure the boy lived 'a clean life'. In other words, he had kept him out of Mafia circles. Therefore Giovanni had not been a courier. This was one of the reasons Balduccio had wanted to meet him: to tell him this in person. It bothered the old gangster to see Giovanni's memory tarnished. But, then, what did those traces of cocaine in the shoebox mean? The coke couldn't have been for personal use, since Giovanni's friends maintained he never took any. Maybe Dolores liked a snort now and then. Then there was what Don Balduccio left unsaid. He never once said the name of his daughter-in-law. And this surely meant something. The silences of Mafiosi often say much more than words could ever do. Another point: Balduccio was convinced that Giovanni couldn't deliver the letter because he had never crossed the straits. In his opinion, he had gone no farther than Catania. But how could he claim this, when the blood in the sink proved that Giovanni had been in Gioia Tauro? Last point: Balduccio, in judging the whole matter to be 'shit' and declaring his unwillingness to concern himself with it, was leaving it up to the law for a precise (but undeclared) purpose. (In the mouths of Mafiosi, the real purpose was always hidden behind another apparent, but false, primary purpose.) Balduccio wanted those responsible for Giovanni's murder to end up in prison after a public trial that would expose their filth and ferocity to everyone. If he had taken matters into his own hands, the culprits would, of course, have paid for their actions, but they would have quietly disappeared, killed by *lupara bianca*. He was, in short, using the law as a refined form of vendetta: the public disgrace.

In conclusion, Balduccio was certain that Giovanni had been killed the moment he learned that the letter had never been delivered. That failure spoke more clearly to him than any hard evidence. Because, if one thought about it, the whole story was full of objects either absent or present. A hand-delivered letter that never arrives. A bouquet of roses that hasn't been picked up by the evening, but which is gone the following morning. The dust that shouldn't have been there, on the little table in the entrance. A rubbish bin that should have contained the remains of a meal but was empty. An unpaid electricity bill. A bloody syringe...

Wait a minute, Montalbano! Stop right there!

The rubbish bin at Via Gerace was made of plastic!

Positive? Positive. And if it was plastic, it couldn't have a rusted bottom. What a colossal moron! What he'd seen wasn't rust, but dried blood! Blood that had leaked out of the syringe when it was thrown into the bin!

Phone Esterina Trippodo in the morning.

He now understood the moves he had to make next. He kept writing.

Call Macannuco, bring him up to date on everything, suggest to him what needs to be done.

As soon as he finished this sentence, he felt a little tired. Tired but satisfied. And he was sure that if he lay down he would fall asleep immediately.

*

He was woken by a noise in the kitchen. He looked at the clock: nine-thirty. *Matre santa*, it was late!

'Adelina!'

'Wha'd I do, 'Spector, d'I wake a you up? You's a-sleepin' like an angel!'

'Could you make me a nice, proper cup of coffee?'

He got up and, instead of locking himself in the bathroom, went into the dining room and dialled directory enquiries. A horrendous, recorded woman's voice answered. In the end the robotess gave him the number he wanted. Before dialling it, he drank his coffee. And before anyone answered at the other end, he had time to revise the times tables for seven, eight, and nine. At last a female voice picked up.

'Hello!'

'Hello, is this Mrs Esterina Trippodo?'

'Who the fuck do you think it would be when you dial my home phone number?'

Always so gracious and refined, that woman!

'Inspector Montalbano here. Do you remember me?'

'How couldn't I? Long live the King!'

'Long live the King! I have a little favour to ask of you, signora.'

'At your service. If we of the same faith don't help one another . . .'

'I need you to go and get the Alfanos' rubbish bin, exactly as it is, and bring it to your place. And for heaven's sake don't clean it! And don't remove the lid. My colleague Macannuco will come sometime today to pick it up.'

'No, Macannuco, no!'

'Please, Esterina, in the name of our common faith.'

It took him a good fifteen minutes to persuade her, all the while cursing inside every time he had to sing the praises of the House of Savoy. Afterwards, he called the station.

'Your orders, Chief!'

'Cat, I'll be coming in late.'

'You're the boss, sir.'

'If Fazio's there, put him on.'

Three times table.

'Hello, Chief?'

'Fazio, is Mimì in his office?'

'No, he went to Montelusa to see Musante.'

'Listen, there's something I want resolved by the end of the morning, but I don't want Mimì to know about it. All right?'

'Whatever you say, Chief.'

'I want you to find me the exact date Filippo Alfano was murdered in Colombia.'

'The records office here must certainly have the death notice.'

'Good. When you've got everything in hand, give it to Catarella. Before the morning's over, I want him to find out, via the Internet, what newspapers there were in Colombia at the time and to get in touch with one of them.'

'Why?'

'Because I want to know the exact circumstances of the death of Filippo Alfano.'

Fazio was silent for a moment.

'I know it won't be easy, Fazio, but—'

'Chief, I think I remember that the person who told me the story of Filippo Alfano also mentioned that the papers here talked about it too.'

'So much the better. In short, one way or another, I want an answer.'

Next, he called Macannuco. And they spoke for half an hour. In the end, they were in agreement on everything except one small detail.

'No, I refuse to say "Long live the King" to that woman!'

'C'mon, Macannù, what the hell do you care? Just say it, and you'll see, she'll open up to you.'

Now he had to prepare his third move, which would be a shot in the dark and therefore the riskiest of all. But if he was on the mark, it would be the one that resolved everything.

'Adelina!'

'Wha's it, signore?'

'Get a piece of paper and start writing.'

'Me? You know I don' write . . .'

'It doesn't matter. Let's do it this way. I'll write something for you on a piece of paper, and you copy it onto another piece. OK?'

He took the paper and wrote in block letters:

I'VE GOT THAT SYRINGE YOU KNOW ABOUT. GUESS WHO I AM AND GET IN TOUCH, AND WE CAN MAKE A DEAL.

'*Matre santa!*' said Adelina. 'Tha'ss a long writing!'

'Take your time. I'm going to the bathroom.'

He stayed in there for almost an hour, purposely taking things slow, and when he came out, Adelina had just finished.

'I'm all asweaty, signore. Jeez, 'at was hard! Whaddya wan' me a do, sign it?'

'No, Adelì, it's an anonymous letter!'

Adelina looked at him with surprise.

'Wha? You's a man o' the law, sir, an' you mekka me write a 'nonymous letter?'

'You know what Machiavelli said?'

'No, sir, I don' know 'im. Wha'd 'e say?'

'He said the end justifies the means.'

'I don' unnastann, I think I go becka the kitchen.'

I GOTTA SYRINCE YOU KNOW ABOUT. GESS WHO I AM AND GET IN TUCH, AND WE MAKE A DEEL.

It was perfect. He took an envelope, put the anonymous letter inside, and sealed it. Then he wrote a short note.

Dear Macannuco,

I want you to send the enclosed letter by express post from Gioia Tauro to the following address: Dolores Alfano, Via Guttuso 12, Vigàta.

Thanks,

Salvo

He inserted the note and letter into a bigger envelope, wrote Macannuco's address on it, and put it in his jacket pocket.

'Goodbye, Adelì, I'm going out.'

'Whaddya wan' me a make a you to eat?'

'Whatever you want. After all, everything you make is good.'

*

He stopped at the first tobacconist's he passed, bought a packet of cigarettes and a priority-mail stamp, pasted this on the envelope, and put it in a mailbox, hoping the postal service wouldn't take eight days, as it usually did, to deliver a letter over a distance of a hundred and twenty miles.

Catarella was so engrossed at the computer that he didn't even notice when Montalbano came in. In the corridor the inspector nearly collided with Fazio.

'Come into my office and close the door,' he said. 'So?'

'I was right, Chief. Filippo Alfano's murder was reported by the *Giornale dell'Isola*. He was killed on February the second twenty-three years ago, at least that's the date the records office gives for his death.'

'And the upshot?'

'The upshot, for now, is that Catarella has accessed the magazine's archives.'

'Let's hope for the best. Any news of Mimì?'

'He's not back yet.'

'All right, thanks.'

But Fazio didn't budge.

'Chief, what's going on?'

'What do you mean?'

'First you turn the investigation over to Augello and now you're conducting a parallel investigation on your own.'

'But I'm not conducting a parallel investigation! I just had an idea that I thought might be useful. Or should I forbid myself to think just because I turned the investigation over to Mimì?'

Fazio seemed unconvinced.

'Chief, I still can't get it through my head that it was just a coincidence that you asked me about Dolores Alfano before the woman came here to tell us about her husband . . . And I can't stop thinking about the fact that you asked me about Pecorini before we knew that he was involved with Dolores. Don't you think it's time you told me how things really stand?'

What a damn good cop Fazio was! Montalbano weighed his options and arrived at the conclusion that the best course was to tell Fazio part of the truth.

'If I asked you about Dolores and Pecorini, it wasn't because of the murder of Giovanni Alfano, but for another reason.'

'What's the reason?'

'I'd found out that Mimì has been carrying on, for over two months, with another woman.'

Fazio snickered. 'Well, knowing him, it's a surprise it didn't happen sooner.'

'Fine, but I discovered that Mimì's lover is Dolores Alfano and that they meet in a house owned by Pecorini.'

'Holy shit! And are they still lovers now?'

'Yes.'

Fazio was speechless.

'And you . . . you . . . knowing this . . . you assigned him the investigation anyway?'

'Well, what's so strange about that? It was the Mafia that killed Alfano, wasn't it? Don't you agree?'

'So it seems.'

'If we suspected Dolores of having anything to do with her husband's murder, then that would change everything, and Mimì would find himself in a difficult position, to say the least.'

'Wait a minute, Chief. Does Inspector Augello know that you know?'

'That he has a lover and that this lover is Dolores? No, he doesn't.'

'I don't get it,' said Fazio. 'The woman seemed so in love with her husband! Was she with Augello even before she began to worry that her husband had disappeared?'

'Yes.'

'So it was all an act she put on with us!'

'Yes, and she's still reciting it.'

'I'm sorry, but I think I'm losing my mind. Why was Inspector Augello so keen on leading this investigation? To do his girlfriend a favour? But at the time we didn't even know who the dead man was! Unless . . .'

'Very good! Unless Mimì himself already knew, because Dolores had told him who she thought the dead man might be.'

'But that means—'

'Wait. Somebody's scratching at the door,' Montalbano interrupted him. 'Go and see who it is.'

Fazio got up and opened the door. It was Catarella.

'I's knockin' wit' my fingernails and din't crash the door!' he said, chortling with satisfaction.

He laid a sheet of paper on the desk.

'Iss a copy o' the arcticle.'

As Catarella left, Montalbano started reading the article aloud.

HORRIFIC CRIME IN PUTUMAYO

Vigatese businessman murdered and dismembered

A fifty-two-year-old Vigatese businessman, Filippo Alfano, was murdered yesterday in his office at Amatriz 28. The body was found by Mrs Rosa Almù, who went there every evening around eight to clean the premises. Upon entering the bathroom and seeing the contents of the bathtub, Mrs Almù fainted. After regaining consciousness, she called the police. Although Filippo Alfano was clearly murdered, it is not known how, since the body was hacked to pieces with extraordinary ferocity. Authorities hope to establish the cause of death after the post-mortem. Mr Alfano, who came to Colombia when he was transferred from Sicily around two years ago, leaves a wife and young son.

'Shall we bet he was hacked into thirty pieces?' asked Montalbano.

'So our murder looks pretty much like Balduccio's follow-up act,' said Fazio.

Montalbano was thinking that, yes, Balduccio had confessed to the murder of Filippo Alfano, but he had neglected that little detail about having had him chopped up into thirty pieces, the same number as Judas's silver coins. That was why he had admitted to the crime, certain that Montalbano would look into it. He had omitted that detail on purpose. Once the inspector discovered the carnage of Filippo Alfano's corpse, he would understand that its repetition was like forging his signature.

'Take this article and put it away somewhere.'

'Shouldn't I show it to Inspector Augello?'

'Only when I tell you to.'

'I'm sorry, Chief, but this article looks to me like proof that it was definitely Balduccio who—'

'Only when I tell you to,' Montalbano repeated coldly.

Fazio put the paper in his pocket, but seemed more doubtful than ever.

'So how should I act with Inspector Augello?'

'How do you feel like acting? Just act the way you always do.'

'Chief, I've still got hundreds more questions for you.'

'So many? We'll have plenty of time for that later.'

'You coming back in the afternoon?'

'Yes, but late. After lunch I'm going home. You can reach me there if you need me.'

*

Lost in all the potential complications of what he had decided to do, the inspector ate so listlessly that Enzo noticed.

'What's wrong, Inspector? No appetite?'

'I've got some worries on my mind.'

'That's bad, Inspector. Eating, like sex, wants no worries.'

Montalbano took his customary stroll, but when he got to the lighthouse at the end of the jetty, he didn't sit down on his rock, but turned back and went home.

*

They had agreed that Macannuco would phone him at four o'clock. The inspector didn't want to be called at the office; there were too many people constantly going in and out of his room. At four on the dot, the telephone rang.

'Montalbano? This is Macannuco.'

'What do you say?'

'You were right on the money. The stains on the bottom of the rubbish bin are definitely blood. Forensics have got the bin now and are checking to see if the blood's the same as in the basin.'

'How long's that going to take?'

'I asked them to be as quick as possible. They assured me they'll have an answer for me by tomorrow morning. What've you done in the meanwhile?'

'I sent you a letter that I want you to post back here to Vigàta. Do it as soon as you get it, it's very important. Did you talk to your prosecutor?'

'Yes, he granted me authorization to tap the phone. They're working on it now.'

'Did you ask him not to say anything to Tommaseo?'

If the public prosecutor for Reggio Calabria mentioned anything to his counterpart in Vigàta, the latter was sure to talk about it with Mimì. And they could make a great big omelette with all the broken eggs.

'Yes. He put up some resistance, but in the end he agreed.'

'Look, I mustn't have any part in any of this, not now, not later, understood?'

'Not to worry. I never once mentioned your name.'

'How'd it go with Esterina Trippodo?'

'She promised to cooperate. She said she's doing it for you.'

'Did you tell her "Long live the King"?'

'Would you please fuck yourselves, you and Esterina Trippodo!'

EIGHTEEN

When the inspector got back to the station around five, Mimì was beside himself.

'It certainly helps the Mafia around here when you've got people like Musante fighting them! Incompetent fucking idiot!'

'Would you please calm down and tell me what happened?'

'I had an appointment with him at nine o'clock. He made me wait till eleven-thirty. We've barely started talking when he's called away. He comes back five minutes later, saying he's very sorry but has to postpone our meeting until one o'clock. So I go out for a stroll in Montelusa and come back at one. He's waiting for me in his office. I bring him up to date on the investigation and tell him that all the evidence points to Balduccio Sinagra ... So what does he do? He laughs. And he tells me that this is old news. He says that some time ago they'd received an anonymous letter accusing Balduccio of having had one of his couriers murdered for selling drugs on his own, and they'd investigated it and come to the conclusion that Balduccio had nothing to do with it. He says it was a trick to throw them off the trail. Fucking idiots! On top of everything else, he says the courier's body was never found. But now it *has* been found, I tell him, and it even has a name: Giovanni Alfano. And you know what he said to me?'

'Mimì, if you don't tell me, how can I—'

'He said that it couldn't have been Balduccio because it was entirely in Balduccio's interest to keep the man alive. And he mentioned some business about a letter that Alfano was supposed to deliver to someone in Villa San Giovanni . . .'

'Did he tell you how they found out about this letter?'

'Yes, it was actually a trap set by Narcotics. They had set things up so that Balduccio would have to get in touch with this person. They were waiting for the letter to be delivered so they could screw Balduccio. But since it never arrived, they decided that Balduccio had nothing to do with Alfano's murder. I don't really get it, to be honest with you.'

'I don't either. What do you intend to do?'

'I'm not giving up, Salvo. I am certain, you realize, absolutely one hundred per cent certain, that Balduccio did it!' Mimì replied wildly.

Poor man! What a state Dolores had reduced him to! She was contributing to the delinquency of a minor police inspector ... She must have been stirring his pot without respite, not giving him a moment's peace.

'When you questioned Mrs Alfano, did you ask her if her husband had ever told her how his father, Filippo, was killed?'

'Yes. She told me that Balduccio had him eliminated with a pistol shot at the base of the skull.'

'And that's all?'

Mimì looked a bit puzzled.

'Yes. One pistol shot, and that's all. Why do you ask?'

Montalbano chose not to answer the question immediately.

'But why didn't Giovanni ever try to get back at Balduccio, if he knew he was behind his father's murder?'

'Dol— Mrs Alfano said that Balduccio wanted so badly to be forgiven by Giovanni, and did so much for him, that in the end he succeeded.'

'Want some advice?'

'Sure.'

'Ask her if she remembers the name of a Colombian newspaper of the time. Then look up the newspaper's archive on the Internet and search for any articles dealing with the killing. Something useful might turn up.'

'You know, that's a good idea! First I'll talk to Dol— Mrs Alfano, and then I'll put Catarella to work.'

'Better not bring Catarella into this,' Montalbano said quickly. 'Everyone who comes into headquarters passes by his cupboard. We should be more careful. Why don't you do the research at home, on your own computer?'

'You're right, Salvo.'

And he was off like a rocket. Dolores was sure to waste some of his time before pretending to remember the name of a newspaper from twenty or thirty years before. And then Mimì would be completely taken up with his research. It was essential that he didn't get any brilliant ideas about moving in on Balduccio in the three or four days ahead.

*

Adelina had prepared him a special dish. Four slices of charcoal-grilled fresh tuna, not over-done, with tiny shelled shrimps on the side, topped with a *salmoriglio* sauce. With his stomach satisfied, and his spirit, too, he sat down at the table and began to write:

Dear Macannuco,

As I feel that the situation is about to tip in our favour, I am writing to explain to you what I think actually happened in the critaru *case. I've already told you, over the phone, about Giovanni Alfano and his father Filippo, who is said to have been bumped off by orders of the Vigatese boss Balduccio Sinagra. Alfano's wife, a Colombian named Dolores, had been living for a while in Vigàta when she began to be courted by a local butcher, Arturo Pecorini — a violent man previously suspected of murder. To cut a long story short, the two became lovers when* the husband was away at sea. At this point Don Balduccio intervened to defend the absent Giovanni's honour. Balduccio was very fond of Giovanni. Word around town has it that he had his father killed because he thought he had betrayed him, only to realize afterwards that he had made a terrible mistake. But this is all rumour, of course, there is no proof that Balduccio ordered Filippo Alfano's murder. At any rate, Balduccio orders Dolores to return to Colombia for a while and forces Pecorini, by means of threats, to move to Catania. Pecorini opens another shop there, while keeping the one in Vigàta, which he puts in his brother's care. Some time later, Dolores returns to Vigàta, and Pecorini too is allowed to come back on Saturdays and Sundays. The love affair between the two appears, to all observers, to be over. In reality, however, this is not the case. The two lovers continue to meet, in spite of the danger. Bear in mind that Pecorini's house in Vigàta is less than fifty yards from the Alfanos'. When Giovanni comes home for long periods, Dolores becomes exasperated. Giovanni is very much in love with her, and when he is with her he makes up for his forced absences, above all sexually. The woman can no longer stand it. And so Dolores and her lover decide to do away with Giovanni, and to have the blame fall on Balduccio Sinagra. It must have been the butcher's idea, a way to have his revenge. Bear in mind that Giovanni knows nothing of the affair between Pecorini and his wife, since Balduccio, at the time, not wanting him to suffer, warned Giovanni's friends not to mention it to him. And so on the morning of Friday, September 3rd of this year, Giovanni and his wife leave for Gioia Tauro in her car. Dolores tells her husband that the day before, a friend from Catania, having found out they were on their way to Gioia Tauro, invited them to lunch. This last point, however, is my own supposition — it's possible Dolores found a different excuse. The important thing is that she convinced her husband to stop in Catania and go to the butcher's place. Don't forget that Giovanni doesn't know that Pecorini was and still is his wife's lover. And so Pecorini takes them to his house and, after lunch, kills Giovanni with a pistol shot to the base of the skull. What you need to do now is ascertain whether Pecorini has a garage. I think that's where the murder took place. And have Forensics check it very carefully. I am convinced they will find traces of Giovanni's blood there. Because that is where Pecorini chopped the victim into thirty pieces, with Dolores's help. Why? Because Dolores has told him the story of Giovanni's father, who was killed with a shot to the base of the skull and then cut up into thirty pieces — which in Mafia ritual correspond to the thirty silver pieces of Judas, the betrayer. And so they do the same, so that everyone will see this as the signature, the cipher, of Don Balduccio, who has had his disloyal courier, Giovanni, executed in exactly the same fashion as his father. After dismembering the corpse, Pecorini stuffs the body parts into a large rubbish bag and heads to Vigàta. He then buries the remains at 'u critaru — in other words, the potter's field, the place where Judas hanged himself. Which is another stroke of genius in the effort to make it look like a Mafia ritual. Dolores, feeling rather exhausted by the whole ordeal, rests for a few hours at her lover's house and then continues on to Gioia

Tauro, where she arrives that night. For proof of this, ask
Signora Esterina to tell you about the bouquet of roses. Then, on
Saturday morning, Dolores pretends to leave for Vigàta. I say
'pretends' because she decides that it's better to do what she needs
to do in the afternoon, when the concierge's desk is closed and
there's no risk of any bothersome visits by him. At the state road
for Lido di Palmi she crashes her car and, while waiting for it
to be repaired, checks into a motel (I'll give you all the details
later). In the afternoon she tells the motel owner she's going
down to the beach, when in fact she returns to Gioia Tauro on
one of the many buses that run during the summer months.
When she gets to the apartment in Via Gerace, she soils the toilet
bowl, opens a bottle of wine and a can of beer, empties them into
the sink, then leaves them in full view on the counter. From
Catania she's brought along her husband's trousers, a syringe full
of his blood, and a little cocaine. She leaves the trousers in full
view on the bed, sprinkles a few drops of blood around the basin
in the bathroom and then covers them (as you yourself told me)
with the soap-dish. Lastly, she opens the trapdoor to the
crawlspace over the bathroom, where she knows there is an empty
shoebox; she takes this and dusts the inside with cocaine, puts it
back, shuts the trapdoor, and then heads back to Lido di Palmi,
taking the bouquet of flowers, which she gets rid of as soon as she
can. In her haste, however, she makes three mistakes.

1) *She throws the syringe, which still contains a great deal of*
   blood, into the rubbish bin;

2) She forgets to clean the dust off the little table in the
   entranceway (she said she had left the place clean and in
   perfect order before leaving);

3) She fails to pick up an electricity bill, and actually pushes it
   under the little table.

When she gets back to the motel, she sleeps, then leaves for
Vigàta the following morning. A few days later, the butcher
sends an anonymous letter to the Anti-Mafia office accusing
Balduccio Sinagra of the murder of a courier who supposedly
betrayed him. In this way he hopes to prompt an investigation.
But Anti-Mafia and Narcotics know this can't be true, because
of the business of the letter Balduccio himself gave to Giovanni,
which the two killers know nothing about and destroy along with
Giovanni's other things. I realize you may have trouble
understanding all this; I promise to explain it all to you when
it's over. Two months after the murder, heavy rains (aided also,
in my opinion, by Pecorini) bring the remains of an unknown
murder victim to the surface. Dolores then comes to Vigàta police
headquarters to cast the first doubt on whether her husband ever
actually boarded his ship. And, indeed, the representative of the
shipping agents informs us that he never did. I succeed in
identifying the corpse by means of a dental bridge that Giovanni
swallowed as he was killed. Incidentally, in my opinion they
disfigured him so that he could only be identified through DNA
testing, thus giving temporal plausibility to Dolores's phony
concerns over her husband's probable disappearance. In short,
from that moment, it is Dolores herself directing our

investigation, adroitly steering it (especially after I turned it over to my deputy) towards Balduccio Sinagra.

It was Musante (who you know) who convinced me that this was the wrong track. And so I went to Gioia Tauro to inspect the scene myself (I didn't have much time, and didn't come to see you, sorry), which gave rise to some doubts and suspicions.

I think what I've told you so far should be enough for now. If Dolores reacts the way we hope, the game is over. You'll have everything you need to interrogate her. And let me repeat again, my friend, that you must never mention my name, for any reason whatsoever, even if you are subjected to torture.

This is what I ask of you in exchange for having given you the solution to a complex case. You can take all the credit yourself, but you must repay me with your silence. I shall fax this letter to the private number you gave me.

Please call me at home, not at headquarters. The best time would be after ten p.m.

Affectionately,

Salvo

Is it an honest letter? he wondered, re-reading it.

Is it a dishonest letter? he wondered, re-reading it a second time.

It is useful to the purpose for which it is intended, and no more, he concluded as he started getting undressed for bed.

*

The following evening, around ten o'clock, came Macannuco's first phone call.

'Montalbano? I got a phone call from Forensics this morning.'

'Yes, and?'

'You hit the nail on the head. The blood at the bottom of the rubbish bin was the same as that found in the sink.'

'You mean *you* hit the nail on the head, Macannù. Congratulations.'

The next evening, Macannuco called again.

'I got your anonymous letter and forwarded it to you-know-who,' he said.

The third night after he had made the decisive move, he was so nervous he didn't sleep a wink. He was getting too old to put up with this level of tension. When the sun finally appeared, he found himself looking out on a beautiful December morning, cold and bright, without a cloud in the sky. He realized he had no desire either to go to the office or to stay at home. Cosimo Lauricella, the fisherman, was busy with his boat on the beach.

'Cosimo!' the inspector called from the window. 'Could I come out with you in the boat?'

'But I'll be out till the afternoon!'

'That's not a problem.'

*

He didn't catch a single fish, but the effect on his nerves was better than a month in a clinic.

*

The long-awaited phone call from Macannuco came two days later, by which time the inspector was seriously unshaven, hadn't changed his shirt, its collar ringed with grease, and his eyes were so bloodshot he looked like a monster in a science-fiction movie. Mimì, too, was no joke: also unshaven and red-eyed, hair standing straight up so that he looked like the advertisement for Presbitero pencils. Catarella, terrified, was afraid to say anything to either one of them when they passed in front of his cupboard, and would only sink down to the floor.

'Half an hour ago we intercepted a very brief phone call from Dolores Alfano to Mrs Trippodo,' said Macannuco.

'What did she say?'

'She merely asked if she could come by tomorrow around three in the afternoon. Trippodo answered, "I'll be waiting for you." And we'll be there waiting for her, too.'

'Give me a call at the station as soon as you arrest her. Oh, and listen, I had an idea about the syringe . . .'

Macannuco liked the idea. Montalbano, however, didn't care what happened to Dolores; his main concern was to keep Mimì out of the whole affair. He had to pull him out of it and keep him busy for the next twenty-four hours. He called Fazio.

'Fazio? Sorry to bother you at home, but I need you to come to my place right now, in Marinella.'

'I'm on my way, Chief.'

When Fazio got there, he was worried and full of questions. He found Montalbano clean-shaven, wearing a crisp new shirt, spick and span. The inspector sat him down and asked: 'Would you like a whisky?'

'To be honest, I'm not in the habit . . .'

'Take my advice, I think it's better if you have one.'

Fazio obediently poured himself two fingers.

'Now I'm going to tell you a story,' Montalbano began, 'but you'd better keep the whisky bottle within reach.'

When he finished his story, Fazio had drunk a quarter of a brand-new bottle. During the half-hour in which Montalbano was talking, Fazio's only comment, which he said five times, was:

'Holy shit!'

The colour of his face, on the other hand, changed often: initially red, it turned yellow, then purple, and then a blend of all three.

'So, tomorrow morning, what I want you to do,' the inspector concluded, 'is this: the minute Mimì gets to the office, you tell him that an idea came to you during the night, and then you hand him a copy of the article.'

'What do you think Inspector Augello will do?'

'He'll race to Montelusa to talk to Tommaseo, claiming it's proof, then he'll do the same with the commissioner and even with Musante. He'll waste the whole morning running from one office to another. You will then throw down your ace, and make things more difficult for him.'

'And then what?'

'Tomorrow evening, as soon as Dolores gives herself away, Macannuco will phone me at the station. I'll call Mimì and tell him she's been arrested. You should be there, too. I can't imagine what his reaction will be.'

*

At six p.m. the following evening, Mimì Augello returned to the office dead tired and in a rage over all the time he'd wasted in Montelusa. But he also seemed worried about something else.

'Has Mrs Alfano called you?' the inspector asked.

'Called me? Why would she do that? Has she called Fazio, by any chance?'

'No, she hasn't.'

He was agitated. It looked like Dolores had left without saying anything. And was keeping her phone turned off. Apparently she urgently needed to go to Catania to talk to Arturo Pecorini.

'And how did it go in Montelusa?'

'Don't get me going, Salvo! What a bunch of imbeciles! All they do is shilly-shally, take their time, and find

excuses. What better proof do you want than that
newspaper article! But I'll be there again tomorrow,
talking to Tommaseo!'

He left, furious, and went into his office.

At seven that evening, Macannuco rang.

'Bingo! Montalbano, you are a genius! When, as you
suggested, Mrs Trippodo let Dolores have a glimpse of a
bloody syringe, Dolores dug her own grave. And you
want some good news? She gave up immediately. She
realized the jig was up and confessed, blaming it all on
her lover, the butcher. Who, incidentally, was arrested
about fifteen minutes ago at his shop in Catania . . . So
there you go. Anyway, bye now, I'll keep you informed.'

'Informed of what? No need to bother any more,
Macannù. I'll learn the rest from the newspapers.'

The inspector took three, four, five deep breaths, to
get his wind back.

'Fazio!'

'Your orders, Chief.'

A quick glance sufficed to communicate their
thoughts. There was no need for words.

'Go and tell Mimì I want to see him, and you come
back, too.'

When the two returned, Montalbano was swaying
back and forth in his chair, hands in his hair. He was
putting on a performance of surprise, shock, and dismay.

'*Matre santa! Matre santa!*' he said.

'What is it, Salvo?' Mimì asked, frightened.

'I just got a call from Macannuco! *Matre santa!* Who would've thought it?'

'Why, what happened?' Mimì nearly yelled.

'He's just arrested Dolores Alfano in Gioia Tauro!'

'Dolores?! In Gioia Tauro?!' Mimì repeated, flabbergasted.

'Yes.'

'What for?'

'For the murder of her husband!'

'But that's impossible!'

'No, it's true. She confessed.'

Mimì closed his eyes and fell to the floor too fast for Fazio to catch him. And at that moment Montalbano realized that Mimì had suspected all along, but had never been able to admit, not even to himself, that Dolores was involved up to her neck in her husband's murder.

*

The day after his arrival in Boccadasse, the inspector had just entered Livia's apartment when the phone rang. It was Fazio.

'How are you doing, Chief?'

'Not great, not bad, just getting along.'

His dress rehearsal for retirement was going well. Indeed that was a typical reply for a retiree.

'I wanted to let you know that Inspector Augello left

today with his wife and son for a couple of weeks' rest in the town where Beba's parents live. I also wanted to tell you how pleased I am at the way you were able to set everything right. When will you be back, Chief?'

'Tomorrow evening.'

The inspector went and sat by the big picture window. Livia would be pleased to hear about Beba and Mimì. Balduccio Sinagra had had his lawyer Guttadauro call him to tell him how pleased the boss was to see Dolores arrested. Fazio, too, was pleased. And so was Macannuco, whom Montalbano had seen on television, being congratulated by journalists for his brilliant investigation. And surely Mimì, who'd been in a pretty nasty pickle, had to be pleased, even if he couldn't admit it to anyone. So, when all was said and done, the inspector had managed to lead them all out of the treacherous terrain of 'u critaru. But what about him? How did he feel?

'I'm just tired,' was his bleak reply.

Some time ago he had read the title, and only the title, of an essay called *God is Tired*. Livia had once asked him provocatively if he thought he was God. A fourth-rate, minor god, she had added. But as the years passed, he'd become convinced he wasn't even a back-row god, but only the poor puppeteer of a wretched puppet theatre. A puppeteer who struggled to bring off the performances as best he knew how. And for each new performance he managed to bring to a close, the struggle became greater, more wearisome. How much longer could he keep it up?

Better, for now, not to think of such things. Better to sit and gaze at the sea, which, whether in Vigàta or Boccadasse, is still the sea.

Author's Note

As is obvious, the names of characters, companies, streets, hotels, etc., are entirely fictitious and make no reference to reality.

Andrea Camilleri

Notes

page 4 — . . . with a *coppola* on his head: The *coppola* is a typical Sicilian beret made of cloth and with a short visor.

page 4 — Totò Riina: Savatore ('Totò') Riina (born 1930) is the former leader of the infamous Corleonesi clan of the Sicilian Mafia and became the *capo di tutt'i capi* ('boss of bosses') in the early 1980s. Riina's faction was responsible for the spectacular murders of the Anti-Mafia magistrates Giovanni Falcone and Paolo Borsellino (both in 1992), crimes that led to a serious crackdown on the Mafia and ultimately the arrest of Riina in 1993. Riina, one of whose nicknames is 'La Belva' or 'The Beast', is known to be particularly bloodthirsty and violent.

page 4 — . . . Bernardo Provenzano for Vice-President, one of the Caruana brothers for Foreign Minister, Leoluca Bagarella at Defence: Provenzano (born 1932), another prominent member of the Corleonesi clan, became Riina's de facto successor until his capture in 2006. Alfonso Caruana (born 1946), with his brothers Gerlando and Pasquale, ran a vast international network of drug-trafficking, shifting their bases from Sicily to Canada to Venezuela and back to Canada by way of Switzerland and London (hence the 'foreign minister' post in Montalbano's dream); he was captured in 1998 and convicted in Canada, then extradited to Italy in 2004, where he had already been twice convicted in absentia, and where he still awaits final sentencing. Leoluca Bagarella (born 1932), another Corleonese and Riina's brother-in-law, was arrested in 1995, ultimately convicted for multiple murders, and is currently serving a life sentence.

page 10 – . . . **a 'white death' – the shorthand used by journalists when someone suddenly disappears without so much as saying goodbye:** Literal translation of the Italian *morte bianca*.

page 18 – **Montalbano recalled having seen something similar in a famous painting. Brueghel? Bosch?:** The painting is *The Blind Leading the Blind* (1568), by Pieter Brueghel the Elder, at the Museo di Capodimonte in Naples. It is inspired by a statement by Jesus in the Gospels (Matthew 15: 13–14; and Luke 6: 39–40): 'Can a blind man lead a blind man? Will they not both fall into the ditch?' (Gospel of Luke)

page 19 – . . . *'u critaru*: Sicilian for *il cretaio*, or 'the clay-field'. From *creta* (*crita* in Sicilian), which means 'clay'.

page 43 – **Don't you like Guttuso?:** Renato Guttuso (1911–1987) was a Sicilian-born painter and passionate anti-Fascist and Communist who rose to prominence after the Second World War.

page 57 – *A joyous start is the best of guides*, **as Matteo Maria Boiardo famously said:** Matteo Maria Boiardo (1440–1494), a poet of the Italian Renaissance who thrived at the court of the Dukes of Este in Ferrara, is best known for writing the chivalric verse romance *Orlando Innamorato*, first published in 1495.

page 72 – **He committed a massacre of *nunnati* – newborns, that is.** *Nunnatu*, Sicilian for *neonato* or 'newborn' (also called *cicirella* in certain other parts of Sicily), are tiny newborn fish available only at certain times of the year. Whitebait.

page 72 – . . . *purpitteddro a strascinasale*: Baby octopus cooked in salted water and dressed with olive oil and lemon juice.

page 72 – . . . *aggravated*, **as the ancient Romans used to say:** From the Latin *ad* + *gravare*, 'to make heavy'.

page 102 – **His eye fell upon a book by Andrea Camilleri . . . a popular version of the Passion of Christ:** Cf. Andrea Camilleri, *La scomparsa di Patò*. Milan: Mondadori, 2000.

page 218 – . . . **another Vittorio Emanuele, Umberto's son, the one known in the scandal sheets for a stray shot he had once fired:** In 1978, when his rubber dinghy was accidentally taken from the docks after a violent storm off the Corsican shore, Vittorio Emanuele IV, banished heir to the throne of Italy, carelessly shot at a man on the yacht to which the dinghy had been attached. He missed his target but mortally wounded Dirk Hamer, a young German sleeping below deck.

page 218 – **As the lady was fumbling with the *napoletana* . . .:** A *napoletana* is a Neapolitan coffee pot consisting of two superimposed cylindrical elements, formerly of aluminium, and a double filter. When the water in the lower part begins to boil, one is supposed to turn the pot over to allow filtration.

page 242 – . . . **the miraculous intervention of Padre Pio:** Pio of Pietrelcina, whose given name was Francesco Forgione

(1887–1968), was a devout priest (Padre Pio means 'Father Pius') reputed to perform miracles. Among other things he 'received the stigmata' and was said by witnesses to have levitated while saying the Mass. Immensely popular during his lifetime, he was canonized by Pope John Paul II in 2002 and remains widely venerated in Italy, particularly in the south.

page 244 – . . . **the arrest of two regional parliamentary deputies of the Centre-Right on suspicion of collusion with the Mafia. While we have, of course, only the deepest respect for the magistrature, we cannot help but note that it moves all too often in only one direction:** The despised Pippo Ragonese is using the same argument as has been made *ad nauseam* by Italian Prime Minister Silvio Berlusconi during his repeated legal troubles: to wit, that the magistrature – the Italian state institution least compromised by the endemic corruption that plagues the other branches of government – prosecutes only politicians of the Right and Centre-Right (in other words, Berlusconi's own coalition) because it is irredeemably 'communistic' and therefore prejudiced against its 'ideological enemies'.

page 255 – **A nice little pact between the Mafia and the 'Ndrangheta:** The 'Ndrangheta is the Calabrian Mafia. In this statement the Mafia is intended to refer specifically to the Sicilian Mafia.

page 260 – . . . **killed by *lupara bianca*:** *Lupara* ('wolf-gun') is the Sicilian term for sawn-off shotgun, formerly the weapon of preference of the Mafia. *Lupara bianca*, or 'white *lupara*', is a term coined by Italian journalists to designate those deaths at the hands of the Mafia where the victims vanish without a trace.

NOTES

page 283 – . . . **hair standing straight up so that he looked like the advertisement for Presbitero pencils:** Camilleri is referring to Italian ads from the first half of the twentieth century that featured the face of a man with spiky hair consisting of pencils standing on end.

Notes by Stephen Sartarelli